THE FIRST THING SMOKING

THE FIRST THING SMOKING

Nelson Eubanks

ONE WORLD

BALLANTINE BOOKS

NEW YORK

A One World Book
Published by The Random House Publishing Group

Copyright © 2003 by Nelson Eubanks

www.ballantinebooks.com/one/

Library of Congress Cataloging-in-Publication Data is available from the publisher upon request.

ISBN 0-345-45178-3

Text design by Susan Turner

Manufactured in the United States of America

First Edition: August 2003

10 9 8 7 6 5 4 3 2 1

For Mel and Marlene for letting me stand so long on the shoulders of giants; their shoulders, that is.

CONTENTS

ACKNOWLEDGMENTS

Writing stories is a taxing, solitary affair you can only undertake after a great many people have given you their time to listen and then sit with you sometimes over many years coaching and teaching, quietly directing you through the various techniques for boiling down people, the world, and the word. The lessons these folks poured into me led me to spin these stories, though the only voice here seems to be mine. Where do you begin and how do you ever end trying to give the true thanks for the wise words and guiding hands? I've had a hard time over the many months figuring out how to say minus them in my life, I'd have come undone or, at the very least, worried myself into quitting. Listing their names on a page of acknowledgments doesn't seem enough, but I guess it's a start.

I'd like to thank my folks, Mel and Marlene Eubanks, for believing in me even when I was sure everything had burned up and blown away. Aunt June for teaching a dyslexic how to read. My grandfolks for putting some common sense in my head, helping me to never quit. Kate Brady, Zack Rogrow, and Anne Barrows for the vision via hard work and fundamentals at the University of San Francisco; Jen Egan, Austin Flint, and Quincy Troupe for their astonishing insight. I'm not sure how to thank Maureen Howard and Binnie Kirshenbaum for showing me how to look harder and deeper at my sentences and thus myself 'cause really, these pushes have made the difference. I'd like to thank my writing group or really my guiding light: Rachel Wenrick and Max Ludington, Gordon Haber and Ben Alsup, from whom the world can expect great things. Mark my words. My agent, Jennifer Lyons, for fighting hard for me over and over again. Her assistant, Katie LaStoria, for doing much of the grueling work that makes things go. I'd like to give a big thanks to my editor at Ballantine, Dan Smetanka, for putting up with my hard head, all the while teaching me. No easy thing. Perhaps the hardest job of all. His assistants Abby Durden for her eyes on the manuscript and Joan Mendenhall for piecing this together. My guitar teacher, Rich Fusco, for lessons that had nothing to do with guitar. Reyna Lingemann for the long and mind-clearing walks through the woods of the Santa Cruz Mountains. The photographer Shannon Brinkman for the pictures and her time, as well as Matt Rudoff for clueing me in on the slow-down-easy-ways of the California life. I'd like to thank Tara Smith for her midnight-hour frank words of advice, Gaby Calvocoressi and Angeline Shaka for their midday frank words of advice. Lots of riddles in this game. Lisa Herbert and the Herbert family: Debbie, Norman, and even Franz. The puzzles of that time are finally coming together and beginning to make sense. Patience. Rachel and the Reinhards: Rick and Judy and Willa. Their words on how to be and move in this world still ringing through my mind as I write this. I'd like to thank Natasha Radojcic-Kane for turning me around and breathing life back into me, pulling me up when for the longest while I couldn't see how far I'd fallen.

I'd like to thank Jo-Ann Townsend for showing me how to steer as good a ship as I possibly could through the many storms, clear and far from the rocks. And not least I'd like to give a double shout at Chef A and Chef B and the Dark Creole King Chef C: Steve McAnulty and super Lee Arnold and the mighty Chuckie White, respectively. Jeff Ross and Big Matt Frances, for you should very much know why. Nicola Fabens, a settling force. Master Peter: look, you're in print. Slovato Montelibano, Maggie McEleney, Sarah DeBacher, Baty Landis, and Eleanor Burke for New Orleans, all of it. Such a soft landing after New York. And perhaps most of all to Kathy Bodnar, wherever you are. One day in Newport, Rhode Island, in her car she looked over at me and said, "You can do this, you really can," and for some odd reason, I could never now in a million years tell you why, I smiled at her and believed.

AVENIDA ATLÂNTICA

THROUGH THE OCEAN MIST THE *POLICÍA* WAVED THE line of headlights forward while standing by the ambulance parked across two of the lanes. He blew his whistle softly, moved cars slowly, leaned in windows with words for those stopping to look for too long. Red and white lights were still spinning from the police cars, from the ambulance, off moving faces, off the cars slowing, now moving along, but there was no sound in any of it. Just the crashing black waves of Copacabana through the swaying palms. Just the big eyes and "ahhs" out of passing cars with bossa nova, samba, and pagode turned down low. Another *policía* diverted traffic on the other side of *Avenida Atlântica* so nobody could see but heads out moon roofs and windows. Next to the two mashed-up cars another *policía* spoke to the two cut-up men, standing in oil and red glass. One man was black. One beige. Their hands were going everywhere. Smell of salt water and gas. Headlights across buttons and knees. A paramedic smoked by himself while the ocean air blew pages of blood-soaked newspaper up here and there. In the headlights the bleeding beige man pointed, now pleaded with his hands in prayer, toward the crumpled scooter, toward the still boy, toward the bleeding black man, toward the white *policía* with baton and cuffs reaching for praying beige hands. The twisted boy's body lay in blood mixed with glass mixed with oil and gas, with a few sheets of the Sunday edition over his face. Blood was soaking through again, but there was lots more newspaper. The beige man got pushed into the back of the police car as the cut-up black man smiled big from the sidewalk near the swishing trees. In the lights the *policía* were brilliant moving traffic along.

MALTA SCHEFFER

Part 1

IT WAS LATE AND WARM, AND MY DADDY SQUINTED AT
the white crumpled paper in his hand and down at the
metal cellar doors and back at the white crumpled paper
and got down on one knee and thump-thump-thumped
the secret knock on the metal doors like the Chinaman at
the stationery store had told us. Puerto Ricans stood like
shadows on the corners and on the stoops and out the project windows, looking this way and that way, leaning and
talking loud and smiling and laughing, so though it was
dark, you could hear them far off into the night. Lights
popped on and peppered the big buildings around us as
merengue and salsa and disco poured out of the lit squares
and dark stoops. The music filled the streets and boys
were getting in their last at bats at stickball, and my daddy
looked up at the closed-up store and blue-and-white sign—
POLLO, CARNE, COCA-COLA, CERVEZA—and down at me
and the metal trapdoors and said, "I don't know, Maceo."

The days were getting longer and warmer as summer
was coming down on the city. School was ending and the
nights were orangy blue over the Hudson, and all the folks
without air-conditioning across the street were out on the

corners and stoops waiting for the cool winds to come down offa the Hudson down a ways, down One Hundredth, and into open windows to help the twirling fans along so folks could lie down without sweating their sheets and get some sleep. The nights were turning orangy pinkish blue over the Hudson, and my classes at private school were finishing, which meant I could slip outta my white world and fade back into my brown one, where nobody had too much more than anybody else, which wasn't so much. White faded to brown, private school went to playgrounds, downtown became uptown, and my mama's lie of Ninety-sixth Street and Central Park West snapped back to the truth of our home on One Hundredth and Columbus with the Puerto Rican projects looming across the street.

As summer drifted on us, down on the playground the stickball games were getting good and long 'cause the scouts from the Spanish Little League were still looking for a missed star or two. Those that hadn't been picked wolfed a lotta loud shit about what they were gonna do to the feltless tennis ball when they were up to bat. All those out in the field that'd been picked made sure we knew we hadn't been as the pink ball zipped and bounced and spun and jumped up at the white, square strike zone spray-painted onto the side of our building. Sneakers screeched and elbows got skinned as those that made it talked about ya mama and ya daddy, ya grandmammy, and what a chump ya were for not being on no team. Those that had been signed wore their hats and team jerseys with their names embroidered in big letters on the back. They wore their hats and team jerseys and Sears blue, blue Toughskins with the reinforced knees 'cause the team-issued pants would get holes instantly from sliding on the playground concrete. As we played Puerto Rican men with cigarettes and cigars leaned on fences among the bushes around the playground, watching, taking notes, speaking Spanish, calling those that were playing well outta the heated games to come and sign with their teams. Somebody'd get called out, and the game would pause and all of us would watch the deals go down as everybody quietly erased the latest Reggie Jackson from the scrub list and added him to that of the Chosen.

I went to a white private school downtown and nobody else did. I was nine and younger and smaller and not on a team, and when I was at bat, nobody let me forget any of it. They called me runt and sissy and white boy and baby and smart-ass, for though school was just getting out for me, the public school had long been out, which meant all my playground friends were in full summer swing. I was the youngest of the large bunch on the playground, but I'd passed all their tests; I could fight, could fight back, didn't cry, didn't get caught, didn't tattle, and could run fast, catch, switch-hit, and play anything well. "Even at six on his Big Wheel," my mama liked to boast, "he kept up with those ten-year-olds on their bikes." It probably wasn't true.

But the Spanish league was different because the games were packed with jeering and cheering fans, and the Puerto Rican coaches and team affiliates watched one another and one another's teams for anything underhanded, for on every Little League game, in the stands and the dugouts, too, fortunes were lost and won.

At my turn at bat in the stickball games I was switch-hitting left and right and cracking the pink ball and getting on base and stealing bases, and I didn't understand 'cause some of the latest Jacksons that'd been signed weren't hitting the ball as far or as often, and as more of them got signed and not me, the good players on the playground eased up on their wolfin' when I was at bat, for they knew what was happening and why I could not be chosen.

Some years back a coach had been stabbed for bringing in a ringer Dominican that was one year past the cutoff. Some fan who'd lost a lotta money because of that boy's hitting found out and lost it and ran down outta the bleachers and let that coach have it. Right in the gut. I was too young. That was against the rules. I was a risk to people's safety. I probably would not make a difference. Nobody wanted to take any chances.

Lights popped on and peppered the projects around us as merengue and salsa and screams and laughs drifted outta the lit squares and offa the stoops, and my daddy got down on one knee and clang-clang-clanged the secret knock on the metal doors like the Chinaman at the stationery store had told us. The trees swayed and the breeze touched our faces and the different dinner smells were in our noses, and my daddy looked at the crumpled white paper and the closed-up store and down at me and the metal doors and said, "Maybe this isn't it." I didn't know what to say, because the Chinaman across One Hundredth knew just about everything and I wanted to play and this was it, and we looked down 'cause there was a clang-clang-clang-clanging coming from the metal doors. We stepped back and my daddy clang-clanged again, and the metal mouth in the middle of the sidewalk opened up. A head popped up and out and his eyes eyed us, and my daddy said, "We want to see Rodrigo." The eyes eyed us and stopped on me, and a hand came up and waved us down. My daddy held on to the sidewalk and cinched his head to the side as he descended the small and narrow stairs. He turned around and said, "Come on," 'cause looking down into the dark, I wasn't so sure I wanted to go. I took a step and then another and heard the Puerto Rican man closing the doors, as the salsa and merengue became dulled and muffled, and I could feel him walking behind me and could see only black in front of my face. I went slowly, trying to feel my hands along the wall, testing each step with a dangled dipped foot, stepping only when I felt the stair beneath me. Near the bottom I could smell the cigarette and cigar smoke as my eyes adjusted to the one lightbulb hanging in the middle of the dark basement. I saw the smoke lingering around the light and the four Puerto Rican men sitting at a round table with their eyes and ears focused on my dad. My dad was talking. There was a little transistor in the corner playing salsa. I heard the men on the radio wailing in their song. I stopped.

I stopped and the man who'd let us down said, "Pardone," and went to the table and sat down on a large fruit box turned on end at the table. It was what they all sat on. I looked around and there were boxes and crates and silver kegs leading all over, going deep into the corners until you couldn't see anything. The floor sloped down, and I looked at the little drain at my feet and saw another near a half-shadowed silver keg and another near one of their sneakers and saw a red baseball sock and a red hat like the four men had on on the floor near a crate and looked on top of another crate and said, "Ahhh." There were a bunch of gray baseball pants next to a pile of red hats next to a couple of stacks of red socks and a long line of gray-and-red baseball shirts with red numbers and large red letters saying MALTA SCHEFFER. The best team in the league.

I looked over and the men were all turned and looking at me, and my dad was saying, "He can hit anything on both sides. He's better than almost all those kids on that playground, you know, you've seen 'em." Four of the men spoke Spanish among themselves, and the man who'd let us down was shaking his head no and talking loud, and the others spoke loud at him, and my dad pulled out his wallet and a bunch of dollars came out and the men all went quiet, watched him. The four men looked at my dad and then at the man who'd let us in who had been shaking his head. My dad put the stack of dollars on the table. The man with a cigar, who'd said nothing, counted the money. He looked at my dad. He smiled. The man who'd let us in started to say something and the cigar man did a one-handed "safe" motion and all went quiet except the salsa playing on the radio in the corner. He looked at my dad and smiled again. He looked over at me and smiled and took out his cigar and in a heavy Spanish accent said, "Come here, Maceo," as he waved me over with his fingers moving rapidly at himself.

"You can hit, huh?"

"Both sides."

"And throw?"

"You've seen me play stickball!"

"We'll teach you and you'll become the next Roberto Clemente, yeah. Rodrigo," he said, "go get the papers. Maceo, go pick a number. Two to five are the smallest."

He looked back at my father and the money on the table, and I went over to the uniforms and he said, "I know a man who will make him a new certificate and nobody will know, and if they ask, we will have the proof. He has done it for me before. With training, your boy will make a fine ballplayer, a fine Malta Scheffer player with some training."

Above ground with my new uniform and the iron mouth in the sidewalk closed, we walked home. My dad laughed and put his arm around my shoulder and said, "Now you'll have to play as good as I told them you could play," and he giggled some more about something I didn't understand.

Part 2

MY MOM LET HER LONG LEGS SPREAD WIDE AND HER arms fall loose in between as she rocked her head back and laughed so you could see her teeth and dimples that came out only during the good times. She looked at me and smiled. "Oh, son, it'll look fine," she said as she tugged and pulled down my uniform shirt and pants. She clenched the sewing needle in between her lips and looked up at me standing on the foldout wood card-table chair, looking down and out of the big living-room window at the yellow cabs and long buses racing down Columbus Avenue. The shirt came down too far on pants too long and baggy, so though I had on red baseball socks that fit, you couldn't see them, for the gray pants passed my socked feet. I stood on the chair feeling the morning sun on my face, smelling the grits simmering and the bacon crackling in the kitchen as my dad tended the stove, singing, "You'll never find," along with Lou Rawls on the record player. The day was gonna be a warm one, and my mom was excited and my dad was all smiles and I was neither smiles nor excited because I'd learned quickly that month baseball wasn't stickball; organized sports with grown-up coaches didn't go by playground rules.

I stood on the chair as sun came down and the buses and cars raced by and my ma tugged and pulled and my dad cooked and sang and the bacon popped and crackled and I went over and over all that the man with the cigar and red hat had been telling and teaching me. He meant to make good on making me a Roberto Clemente; elbow up, get in front of the ball, get down on the ball, the ball doesn't hurt when it hits you, mitt open, no swinging on the first pitch, watch the spin of the pitch, concentrate, watch the batter's stance, take a hop to be on your toes, always hit the cutoff man, take your time, pay attention, don't lead too far, round third like this, keep your concentration, attack the ball, level swing, square for a bunt, it doesn't hurt, well, only for a little does it hurt. It all swished and sloshed around my head as I went over and over his words, sometimes remembering all, sometimes less, sometimes not understanding at all.

The man with the cigar, the coach, had at one time come very close to the big leagues. They didn't like too many Spanish on their teams then, he'd say. He had played many years and was patient but pushy. He knew his stuff, so as to make my pop very pleased with my progress in the fundamentals. My pop had been very good and had played for many years, coming very close to the big leagues till he broke his leg his last year in college. My dad's youngest brother, Uncle Marvin, who now lived in Brooklyn, had been very good and had made the big leauges by hitting seven outta twelve balls outta Three Rivers Stadium in

Pittsburgh. The Pirates wanted him, but something happened and he didn't want to play professional sports, which nobody, especially my pop, could understand.

The coach said I reminded him of himself when he was my age. My pop said my swing looked just like Marvin's when he was at that age. Uncle Marvin outta Brooklyn said again and again if I kept working on the fundamentals, I'd be the best Watson ballplayer of all.

My uniform fit good but I didn't care 'cause I was on the bench and had not played as the sixth inning rolled on and the other team cracked another hit. There was the smell of the hot dogs and sauerkraut, and hot pretzels with mustard, and the trees in Central Park swished and swayed with the breeze as the man with the cigar and red hat puffed away and screamed out the other corner of his mouth and three times trounced upon his hat on calls going the other way. His red hat was dusty with infield brown dirt. People cheered and jeered and pointed at me sitting alone at the end of the bench, dangling my feet back and forth. They didn't touch the ground unless I sat near the edge of the bench and really tried. I kept my head down, watching my white-and-light-blue new Nike canvas tennis shoes getting dirtier and dirtier as I occasionally kicked up a plume of infield dirt with my toes for no good reason. The old Spanish men were there, and mothers and wives and girlfriends and the men with red hats from the basement and the next teams getting ready to play, eating hot dogs and popcorn and pretzels and Italian shaved ices, with babies sleeping on laps and shoulders of women with other kids not too much younger than me running around playing freeze tag behind the bleachers.

There were cheers from the other side's set of bleachers

and lots of talk in Spanish on our side, with the men gesturing with outstretched hands and palms slapping heads and eyes occasionally rolling up to heaven. The man with the cigar, *chomp,* chomped it as he screamed "Polla" and "Puta" as strikes came our way and long balls went against us and my new white canvas shoes got dirty red brown swinging back and forth kicking up dust.

One, two, three, we were out and the man with the cigar said, "Dio," and some other things and shook his head back and forth and looked over to the end of the bench and said in his heavy Spanish accent, "Maceo, ala derecha," which I'd come to learn meant "right field." I saw my mitt against a bat against the steel wire fence. I grabbed it and ran as fast as I could to the outfield. My ma stood up and screamed, "Go, Maceo," and clapped as I waved to her from right field.

Seemed like soon as I was out there, our team was back on the bench. Somebody was up and got a hit. There were cheers. Somebody else cracked on and louder cheers. Three or four more, *crack, crack, crack, crack,* and the men on the other bleachers were making the hand gestures and eyes to God, and the women with babies on their shoulders on our side were up and cheering now, so their babies were awake and crying, and the men were nodding in approval, showing one another the last swing and flight of the ball with their hands. It was the top of the eighth and it was my turn and people were pointing and laughing and the first pitch came a strike and the second a ball, and the third and I saw the laces spin just like he said and *crack,* cheers, and I watched it rise over the second baseman's head and "Run, Maceo, run," I heard my mom say above it all and I was off and on first. The coach was clapping and my ma was jumping and cheering and the men from the basement were watching very closely, for the other team was not supposed to be this good, but we were within one run now and might make everything all right and square with the bets they'd made.

Fat Black Charles came up and he must've got his weight behind it. The ball soared. I went as fast as I could, rounding the bases just as the cigar man had said, and the people on our side went wild, standing, waving their hats and fists and red-and-white Malta Scheffer pennants in the air, chanting, "Malta," clap, clap, clap, clap, "Scheffer," clap, clap, clap, as Fat Black Charles just trotted slow and easy around third. The ball was gone way over the fence.

Our rally was done and we were ahead by one and all eyes were on the coach at the mound 'cause our pitcher had just hit a kid and his arm was spaghetti but we didn't have anybody else who could throw nearly as hard. He threw one high and another too low and another with one hop off the ground and our coach was back out again, and I don't know what he said to him.

The coach came out again and I smelled the hot dogs and sauerkraut from the hot-dog cart and thought of lunch and how good it'd be to have a hot dog and heard the kids behind the bleachers laughing and screaming, playing freeze tag, and saw a baby girl stumble and fall on the paved walkway, with the mother quickly going to her rescue. It was hot and they'd only mowed the grass on the other side of the paved walkway and I looked down at the dandelions and wondered why. They were big and tall and yellow and I went after them, kicking their heads right off, *whack,* and away they flew up and they were gone in the breeze. Then I jumped up and crunch-crunched the stems and then I was doing 360 spins on yellow heads and green stems and I tried it with my eyes closed around and around and around on one of those dandelions and then there was a crack from somewhere.

There was a crack and the man with the cigar was screaming, "Maceo! Maceo! Puta, Dios, Maceo!" and the people were all over everywhere screaming and women were shrieking and babies crying, the men in hats from the basement were standing half up, hands mushing red hats on heads, and everybody was pointing this way and that way in my direction and I spun around and around and shrugged my shoulders at the people as the boy who was on first rounded second and the center fielder was screaming, "THERE, THERE, THERE, the ball, Maceo," as he ran toward me and I saw the ball and ran at it, got there first, grabbed it, and they say the cutoff man was there but I saw only Fat Black Charles with his mask off at home and I threw the thing hard as I could, getting everything I had in me into the throw, and the ball loped up high in the air over the cutoff man's head, dropping, dribbling, rolling barely past second base, where nobody stood. The boy who'd hit it touched third. Our first baseman ran to the ball and the pitcher ran to the ball and they got to it about the same time but it didn't matter 'cause the boy was being congratulated already by his teammates spilling out onto the infield around him and home plate.

People were still on their feet and the man with the cigar, his eyes were real big and his hat was mashed on the ground. The people on our side of the bleachers were quiet and the men shook their heads 'cause we'd lost bad and they'd lost money. Our players all walked with heads down back to the bench, throwing their mitts and kicking the dirt, and I didn't want to go back there and see any of them, not for nothing did I want to see their faces, their eyes, how they'd look at me like I was a little kid who couldn't play.

I was looking around wondering where I could go to and I don't know how my dad got there, but he was there with me out in the outfield. He picked my mitt up off the grass. He held my mitt, looking down at me, sitting cross-legged on the ground.

"It's all right, son, it's all right," he said, 'cause I guess I was crying.

And he stopped, sat down next to me, looked over, and smiled, putting his arm around me as my mom was walking toward me fast past the bleachers, her hands full with a sauerkraut hot dog and a pretzel with lots of mustard just the way I liked it.

OLINDA

THE MANDOLIN PLAYER HOPPED A LITTLE, PLUCKING
rolling sounds as the tambourine player banged it against
his swaying hips as they intertwined a melody among the
boom-boom-booming of the tallest of the three's big bass
drum. Though a white sand beach, a breeze, and an ocean
full with waves, many stood hot, shoulder to shoulder so
you couldn't see the sidewalk, on the opposite corner. The
buses arrived when they wanted to, but from no other
stop did buses go to Olinda. It was still Carnaval time in
Olinda. The sounds of the three were heard throughout the
throng. Everyone moved: some their shoulders, some their
hips, some their hands above their heads, others just their
torso with bouncing feet. There were many dark bodies
and many shades and no man wore a shirt, and the women
bikini tops, and all had shorts, all flip-flops, all sheens
from the sweating from the heat from the dancing from
the sounds. Everyone moved and moved differently, hearing their own brand of the beat. Everyone moved and
moved differently, but from afar the mass moved as one.

The three playing smiled and laughed with one another,
and the crowd, as the musicians twisted and swayed,
smiled now, too, and men grabbed women, and all sam-
baed and moved more and the Brazilian summer sun came

down and the sweat came down and smiles went throughout. Movement, smiles, sweat. The sweat ran down in streams from the upper bodies, making dark half-moon shapes on the tops of the tight cotton shorts and bikini bottoms and soccer shorts. The whole crowd moved and we moved and the musicians played and the boom-boom-booming drum and the twangs of the mandolin and the rings of the tambourine, and a bus came and dancing stopped and the throng rushed at the still-moving bus and the three musicians held on to the back but fell off, scratching themselves, and their instruments rolling around, scraped knees, stomachs, shoulders, blood mixed with gravel.

The pack was on the bus, climbing and screaming through all the windows, brown sweating bodies squishing against one another, pushing at the front door, many up on the roof, many twisting through the sun roof. The bus was surrounded and then the bus was full. The bus driver screamed in Portuguese. He closed the door. The bus left slowly. It leaned over to the right so the body there nearly touched the ground. A few hung on the back. Some stood on the roof. The bus motor made loud noises and then the bus was gone. The mass moved back and up and over the curb, onto the sidewalk. The three musicians brushed the gravel off their wounds. They checked their instruments.

The mandolin player pulled a bottle from his pocket, turned it around a few times, opened it, drank, smiled, drank again, passed it to the tambourine man, who smiled, drank, smiled, and on to the drummer, who leaned his head all the way back, tipping the bottle on his lips so its mouth kissed his own and his eyes searched only Brazilian sky. He wiped his mouth. He threw the bottle into the street. He grinned. They all grinned. Then the mandolin player began hopping a little, plucking rolling sounds as the tambourine player banged it against his swaying hip as they intertwined a melody among the boom-boom-booming of the tallest of the three's big bass drum. It was Carnaval in Olinda, a bus was sure to come.

MY FRIEND NIGEL

WE HEARD THE CLICK, CLICK, CLICK OF HER HIGH HEELS
on the sidewalk through the morning mist above the
apartment ACs, over John Coltrane's "Summertime" playing soft on the car radio, long before we caught sight of
her red boots, fat legs, tiny bra, bouncing boobs, wiggling
belly, and short, short, tight black booty shorts that flashed
her flabby white ass each time she click-click-clicked, moving fast toward the Hudson down One Hundredth Street,
where we'd been stuck in line for gas since six o'clock, hoping to beat the Jersey Shore traffic over the G. W. Bridge.
Nigel nudged me in the ribs, smiling, staring, as my cousin
Charles and all the other heads of the men standing outside their cars turned slowly, watching her moving quickly
through the heavy heat down One Hundredth, nobody doing nothing particular besides a few head shakes, a couple
of chuckles, and one short, shirtless, rolly old Puerto Rican
man saying real loud, "In this neighborhood, *my* neighborhood," looking around to catch the eye of anyone close
enough to hear who might be biting on this hot day that
was going to boil us all. My daddy sat slumped in the front
seat, fanning himself from time to time with the sports section of the day-old *Saturday Daily News*, humming along
with McCoy Tyner playing the "Summertime" melody on

the piano. "Christ, Maceo! You, too, Nigel!" He turned. "Stop staring at the poor woman—turn round, now—know better than that." But he didn't say it like he meant it for real, and we pretended like we hadn't heard nothing and watched and watched her naked booty sneak out and shake in those short shorts from the back of the car with our knees sticking to the warm plastic covers over the warm beige vinyl seats, us giggling and whispering what we'd do with her if she was in our bed late at night and our parents weren't around, us watching, watching her till all we could make out was the black and red and white of her shifting body going up Riverside Drive, up past One Hundredth and First, up toward Harlem, while the man on the radio told us in a deep voice which license plate numbers could go and buy gas on this odd day, the seventh of July, a scorcher for the record books.

My daddy didn't like to wait till the last minute to get his gas during this crunch laid on us by I-something or another country farther east or middler east than China, where the Chinaman who knows everything and owns the stationery store across the street comes from, but my pops had promised to take us to the beach and you could already feel the heat wrapping all around us thick, making the backs of our necks gritty, sweat on our foreheads and bellies and armpits, my daddy and I through our matching white tank tops, Nigel with drips of water dropping from his stinky pits down his caramel body, making half-moon shapes on both sides of his red swim trunks. When it was hot like this, not to go over to Jersey to the beach meant to stay inside with the air conditioner all day watching golf or baseball or bowling and drinking apple juice with ice or something, and nobody but my mama, who couldn't stand the heat for nothin', wanted that on these nasty, steamy, sunny summer Sundays.

My cousin Charles had pulled his long legs up onto the chrome bumper, moved his skinny body over into the bit of shade making its way onto the curb side of the trunk of the car. He kept starting and stopping some song I couldn't make out that my daddy had just shown him on the harmonica two days ago. He stopped and started and cursed and started, while looking out onto the still Hudson. I could see his bony fingers fluttering back and forth, up and down, all over the harmonica. When he stopped, you could see the rounding dark lines of dirt beneath all his nails.

Nigel and I swiveled around and squished back down to finish our third game of war. We all hoped the other gas pumps would open up on Ninety-sixth so the gas line would start moving faster and we could get some air moving through the windows to cool us down a little bit, maybe even get down past Seaside to the boardwalk so we could ride on the roller coaster my daddy liked and always took us on for the view, he always said, for the waves and nice Atlantic Ocean view.

I flipped a king of clubs to Nigel's last card, the four of diamonds, and opened up the door and got out and started jumping up and down, screaming, "I won, I won," sliding into the two-step victory dance-shuffle Nigel had just finished making up last game, and he started yelling, "Cheater, cheater," as he musta looked down and seen the batch of kings and aces of the same blue-and-white sailboat deck we were using that I'd forgotten I'd stashed for insurance under my feet. My daddy looked over at me dancing the two-step and then down at the cards on the backseat floor and then over to Nigel, now out of the car, grabbing me, trying to make me stop doing the war victory shuffle, Nigel yelling, "Cheater, cheater," as I smiled and giggled and my pop started laughing, so the whole big beige Buick LeSabre started shaking with his big-belly-quaking, eye-squinting, hand-squeezing-the-life-outta-the-armrest laugh. Charles stopped and looked back at me dancing. "Nigel, you a fool lettin' that little boy beat you bad as he does! Boy's nine years old, and what are ya, fifteen?" and "Fuck you!" Nigel said loud, holding the pink ball all up cocked in the air like he was gonna throw it, and before ya could say boo, Charles had swooped down and smacked Nigel across the mouth hard with the harmonica. Nigel didn't cry. He did let the ball drop to the street so he could hold his jaw with both hands, but you could tell a smack like that musta hurt real bad. Charles stood over Nigel and smiled a little and patted him on the back easy and went over up on the bumper and sat just like before but inspecting his harmonica now. Nigel rubbed his jaw and then looked up mean over at Charles and then over at me like that, like he was gonna try and do something. Charles grinned. "Next time I'm gonna beat ya ass and won't matter if the president of the United States is standing 'round, ya see. And don't let me hear nothing 'bout something happenin' ta Maceo, 'cause if I even think ya thinkin' it, I'm gonna grab ya and beat ya stupid." I took a step back and smiled at Nigel. My daddy had his head turned and was just humming the piano part soft, fanning, fanning himself, looking out the other front-seat window like he hadn't seen or heard nothing, though we all stopped and waited a few moments more to make sure 'cause you never could be too sure with him.

Nigel stooped down and grabbed the ball and put it back in his pocket. Charles looked at the back of my daddy's head and then back at us and smiled at Nigel and started up on the parts of the song he knew, trying to keep time with my slowed-down war victory dance two-step, all the while me looking around at the folks staring at me, adding my own modifications so as to make sure Nigel couldn't get too, too mad at me and want to get me more, saying I'd stolen all his new dance completely.

Around ten o'clock the line started moving a little bit, and my daddy tried to turn the car over and nothing happened. He looked out on us in the street playing handball against some building with the pink rubber ball Nigel always carried in his pocket, sweat now glistening on our legs, head, and arms. The car went *wa, wa,* and we stopped and watched and the car went *wa, wa, wa* again and stopped and "Goddamn thing," my pop said. "We're gonna have to push it, Charles," and my cousin snarled, stopped playing the harmonica, and put it in his pocket. My daddy looked out at us looking at him and, "Why don't you boys go on home and get washed up and wait for us there. We're gonna push it through and come and pick you up, and if it's not too late, I'd still like to go. Nice to get down there and stay awhile, wait for the heat to calm a little." Nigel and I lived in the same building a few subway stops up the way.

Nigel smiled at Charles.

"You two can go and pick your mother up some eggs and juice and things while you're at it and get some pizza or something for lunch for yourselves," and he passed me a brand-new twenty-dollar bill. Nigel's eyes got big. Nigel didn't have no daddy. I looked at my pop, who was smiling at me. I looked over at Nigel. I held the bill by the ends and snapped it twice and grinned a little at Nigel. Nigel stuck out his lip.

My pop looked down at me and frowned, then patted my shoulder. "Know better, Maceo. *Two* of you take that money and go and get your pizza over to Sal's or something, and then get them groceries at Red Apple and go straight home, and we'll be there before long."

We both nodded and took off up One Hundredth, following the long line of multicolored cars all the way down to Ninety-sixth right near the underpass where the Indian gas-station man with a dirty white turban on his head was running around alone, checking this, going inside there, moving that over, squeegeeing windshields, closing gas caps, pumping, pumping, taking money, adding dollars to his big wad of green closed with a thin rubber band, now trying to make this one white man in a red Cadillac back up, waving his hands for him to back up, back up, saying, "Shit, shit," all along, now going inside his booth, deep inside to the back of the garage inside the big white brick building, and now coming out, placing a cardboard sign with big black letters saying OUTTA GAS on the other pump he musta just opened up, or maybe that'd been open too long. Nigel threw me the pink ball and I threw it back to him and he looked less mad, a lot better now that we'd moved away from Charles, and he walked over real close to me. "We're never gonna make any beach today."

"No?" I said.

"Look at all them cars."

"Yeah."

"You think he's gonna just get up there like that and we're gonna go?"

"We're gonna go to the beach today," I said.

"Get that out ya head. We're not going anywhere. He's gotta get some gas no matter what time it is, and lookit"—he pointed for me—"that pump is out, and look at all them cars. It's gonna take a long while till ya pop's turn comes with just that one pump, and by that time it'll be too late to do any fuckin' thing." Nigel rubbed his jaw.

"You don't know."

"I know," Nigel said, starting to walk up Ninety-sixth toward the pizza parlor slow, sweating all over from our run. "We should do something fun today anyways." Nigel was only a little bigger than me but three years older, twelve to my nine. He always had ideas.

On the corner of Broadway and Ninety-sixth in front of Sal's Pizza, I started to walk into the warm tomato-sauce smell, clapping my hands, rubbing 'em together real hard and quick like my pop did, come good food close to dinnertime. Seeing the bubbling pepperoni Sal had just pulled out of the big metal oven on the worn wooden spatula with not a nobody standing in line, I wanted to spend all the money and eat it all.

"Where ya going?" Nigel said.

"Eat."

"I thought we were gonna do something today."

"I didn't say that," I said.

You could feel the rumble of the 1 below our feet, coming from One Hundred Third down the tube to the Ninety-sixth Street station, and Sal looked at me, recognized me.

"Wanna slice?" he asked, and Nigel looked at me. "Let's go do something fun downtown," and then, "We can go do all that ya daddy said downtown," smiling at me, and we heard the train roaring to a halt and I smiled at Nigel and we took off down the steps and slipped underneath the big yellow turnstiles and went racing down the stairs and flying up the middle ones, skipping two steps at a time, and down to the last car and sliding through the just-closing doors, sticking our heads out the windows, laughing at the token booth man who'd been shouting what he was gonna do when he caught us, waving his black-gloved fist at us the whole time.

The train rocked and swayed back and forth, and all the windows were down but the air was close and hot and nasty, so you didn't wanna take a breath, but hardly anybody was on and Nigel threw the ball at me hard from the other end of the train as I train-surfed and grabbed a silver pole to help me jump up high and outta the way of the incoming pink rubber stickball. I grabbed it rolling slow and wobbly back off the back door and aimed at Nigel, who was ducking and bobbing and weaving trying to get outta the way of what he knew was coming straight at him. I wound up and threw it like we do pitching on the playground playing stickball. It went hard and off the ceiling and bounced off another silver pole and hit the sleeping, smelly, stretched-out, raggedy, drunk bum right in the head and he jerked up straight for a moment and went back to sleep, mumbling fast, muffled things about the Lord Jesus, Lou Rawls, and getting his two freebies out some sweet-ass Juanita from uptown Newark who'd stolen his favorite golden Nikes. We both fell onto the rows of empty seats right near us and pointed and laughed and laughed, holding our bellies, pretending we were the stupid-ass bum, jerking straight up like he'd just done, while mumbling and giggling about Lou Rawls and Newark sweet-ass Juanita who'd stolen some golden shoes. The train stopped short at Forty-second Street and Nigel ran over and looked at the sleeping bum. "Looks just like Charles," he said, and wound up and threw the ball real hard at the bum's forehead and smacked him across the face, and then I said, "Just like Charles," and running right behind Nigel, I got into my second position and punched the dirty bum real hard right in the nuts like how they taught me to do in my judo class, and he sat up, holding his balls, screaming, "What the fuck, you motherfuckers. I'll get you, motherfuck," as the door closed slowly and his face pushed up against the bottom window, looking at us two laughing at him, giving each other five, to the back side, and then slipping into our war victory shuffle, extra special with some ass shaking straight up in the air, with a quick turn and two fuck-you fingers for him so he could see it all real good as his mouth went wider and faster and the train jerked a moment and started off easy and then slowly sped away.

We ran upstairs to Forty-second Street and none of the lights were on like the last time I was there with my parents. It was a lot bigger than I remembered. Thousands of cars honking and going this way and that way, cutting one another off, running red lights, windows open, people screaming and cursing at one another, people moving, moving, tourists looking up and pointing, the men with the three shells on the standing fruit boxes looking around for suckers. Some older black kid on red roller skates with big yellow wheels, with red-and-white-striped tube socks pulled up high to his knees, held on to the bumper of a taxi, bending down real low so the cabbie couldn't see him in the mirrors. Smart. It was hot. We waved at him as another car passed him, and he nodded at us and looked forward and crouched lower before quickly disappearing and appearing quick behind the rows and rows of parked cars. "That boy looked just like Charles," Nigel said, smiling, as we walked to the corner and watched the back of the skater's blue shiny shorts and white baseball hat, his long, sweating arm stretched all the way out holding on to the bumper. "Just like Charles," Nigel said. "Just like Charles," I said, laughing, thinking of long-legged Charles falling all over himself trying to roller-skate. Roller-skate. A bus was going down the other side, across the street. "You wanna hook on the back?" Nigel asked as it came to a stop behind three cars inching, creeping forward, waiting for their red light to turn green. A street cleaner was coming right where we were standing in the street looking and thinking on hooking the bus, and we jumped back to the middle of the sidewalk and smiled at each other for not seeing that coming sooner as the bristles whirled and spun, kicking up wind and dirt, as the thing had stopped near us for some reason, as the light turned green on the other side of Broadway and the three cars and rumble of the bus engine moved fast and away downtown. Nigel looked around, frowned. "Come on," he said, "I know a good place."

We walked a little ways down toward Eighth Avenue and then turned right around and walked straight back to the mouth of the station on Forty-second, where we'd just come up. We looked around. "This way," Nigel said, and we went over a few blocks toward Madison, Nigel slowing and looking in the windows of every shop to see if this was it, and finally he shook his head, frowned, looked up at the sky, looked down Forty-ninth, smirked, and made a right and then down some more that way and we came to a stop in front of a big newspaper/magazine store.

"What we gonna do?" I asked, and Nigel just smiled and said, "Lemme hold that money, now."

"I'm not dumb."

"Come on and lemme hold that money, 'cause it'll be safer. I don't got time to argue, now! If we gonna do this, I need to hold some of the money, is all."

"Need to get your own money from your own goddamn pop."

"You shut the fuck up about that, Maceo, or I'll knock you on your ass."

Nigel looked at me with his teeth clenched. We both knew Charles wasn't around.

On the corner a little ways away was the yellow-and-blue umbrella of the Sabrett hot-dog man, him flapping and smacking the little metal doors on the top of his cart, putting his buns away here, stocking up drinks in the cooler section there, every now and then looking up to see if any customers were coming, looking to see if anyone was sneaking up on him. I walked back down and smiled at him and got two hot dogs with the works—onions, relish, the orangy red stuff, everything the way my pop always told me not to do. I got two Tahitian Treat sodas like my mom didn't like me to have 'cause the sugar, she said, ruining on my teeth. I came back and gave Nigel a dog and a soda and seven dollars, while keeping the ten for myself.

"Think I'm stupid," I said, and he smiled at me.

We ate 'em quick and washed them down fast and wiped our hands, back and front, on our shorts. Nigel said he was gonna have to sneak in 'cause the creamy brown guy with the double chin and dark, dark Bo Diddley glasses like the pictures on my pop's album covers, the creamy guy up at the clear glass counter, might get pissed 'cause Nigel didn't have a shirt on and was sweating like a pig, which was true. Nigel wanted me to go first. "Distraction," he said. "Like *Get Smart,*" he said. *"Get Smart,"* I said.

I walked slow up to the counter, and the fat creamy black man was playing Bill Evans's version of "Blue in Green" like my pop liked to listen to at home, come Sunday evenings right before our early supper. He had that "Blue in Green" going soft, mixing with the whir of two small fans clipped on the shelf right behind him, the shelf loaded with five big glass jars of red and yellow and blue and green and white marbles, the fans humming along, rotating back and forth, back and forth, blowing air on him from two sides to keep some of the heat and sweat down a little. Leaning my head over the counter, I saw he had a small black-and-white TV tucked down in the corner with a long, straightened-out hanger antenna and some tinfoil bunched and crumpled on top and across, making a giant silver T. He had the Yankees game on with no sound. "Help you?" smiling at me, leaning his big roly body across his counter, and when one of the fans blew on him from the side, I could feel his warm air, could smell the sour mildew on him like my washcloths I used for too long, hanging crusty and dry in the bathroom, and "You need anything, boy?" and the fan blew the smells of that mildew and the fat man's singed dyed light brown hair, all straight back conked and greased, and I looked at him and he had a small orangy red sore like the hot dog stuff, had that sore right below the bottom black rim of those dark glasses. The creamy man stood up offa his high chair and looked down at me. "Ya want something here?" he asked a little louder, and I smiled at him. "Ya got any spearmint gum or Juicy Fruit or somethin'? Ya know, my pop likes to listen to this stuff," and he looked over to where the bubble gum was right in front of me and then outside.

"Where ya parents?"

"At home watching the Yankees like you."

"Right there," he said. "Can you see the gum there, boy? Lookit, can ya see it?" pointing, and I looked straight ahead, straight into his glass counter, looked straight at his long line of many, many different-colored shades of brown cigars, and many, many different kinds of girlie playing cards, some with fat ladies on 'em, some skinny ladies, some had ladies in bikinis with big boobs, some smiling redheads and others blondes with their tongues out on their lips, looking and winking at me, and "Smile," he said, and I looked up and a bright flash and I couldn't see and then I could and he was standing waving a Polaroid picture by the fan, saying, "I got some nice jazz albums in back. You say you like jazz—I got some good albums I'll give you for your pop, he'll love it, if you want to come and take a look at what I got in the back, stacks of jazz. Gum's right there, you can have it free," and I looked down, following his still-pointing finger, and smiled, leaning down to inspect the gum, trying to delay, trying to make a little more time, just like on *Get Smart*. "I can have any album I want?" fingering two packs of yellow Juicy Fruit, and a pudgy palm stroked my Afro real soft and slow, curling banana fingers crawling on the back of my neck, and "Ummmmm, nice, real," and I slipped back, smacked the hand off my neck, and looked at him. He sat his big body back down and laughed and leaned way forward so his big belly lay on the glass counter. He pulled his dark glasses up off his eyes and rested them on top of his light brown hair. He looked at me. He had blue eyes. Milky blue eyes. He took the glasses off and laid them down on the counter next to his Polaroid camera. He looked down at the picture of me lying on the glass counter. "Nice," as he began smiling. He looked out front and turned to me. I looked at him and he leaned forward quietly, lazy big arm stretching toward me, fingers uncurling gently, gently, growing, stretching, reaching to get hold of my arm, and like in slow motion, like them basketball players do during them basketball games on TV, I stepped back easy, not jerking or jumping, just slip-sliding back outta his long reach. He pulled his hand back slow, put his palms flat on the glass. He had dark lines of dirt beneath all his nails. He smiled and leaned back in his chair. He leaned back and turned and grinned at a fly ball on the TV. "Got money on this game, on the Yankees. Like the Yankees? Bet you like the Yankees, got some nice Yankees stuff back there, got some jazz we can listen to and you can have any album I have back there, for your father, for free, just come and pick it out. He'll be excited," smiling wide, so you could see the little dimples in his big cheeks, his teeth yellowing bad like my crazy uncle Raymond's, who smokes all the time, even during Christmas dinner when my grandma asks him a thousand times not to. I walked, turning looking at him from time to time to make sure he kept his fat ass behind the glass, didn't sneak up on me from behind and grab me like Charles would sometimes do when he wanted something. He grinned at me each time I looked back, and outside Nigel was nowhere to be seen, so I knew. "Just a few more things," I said to urine-yellow grinning teeth, and one of the fans turned and the top of the owner's light hair rustled like a playground pigeon's feathers in a wind, along with the dark blue short sleeve along his right flabby arm of his big golf shirt. I stepped back some. It was hot. I tried to keep my arms out far away from my body. The fans turned away from me again and warming still air, rising, standstill heat. The whole store smelled like right after when my mama burns bacon bad in the frying pan come Saturday mornings sometimes and the washcloth mildew all crusty, all mixed in with the hot heat boiling us all, making my neck feel sticky, grimy. I wiped my forehead with my arm. I pulled my tucked-in tank top out and up to my head and wiped it again.

I walked up and down the long aisles, trying to breathe out of my mouth, up and down the rows and rows of magazines about bodybuilding and cameras and cars and decorating and gardening, and down and up the aisles covered with magazines with little girls and high school girls and older ladies all prettied up with makeup and lipstick, me looking for where Nigel had hidden himself. Down the last aisle, over in the back corner, Nigel was squatting down with his back against the wall with a *Sports Illustrated* already open. His eyes had gone wide like when he saw my twenty. I walked toward him. "We come all the way down here for this stuff, 'cause we coulda gone right cross the street to the Chinaman for . . ." and I stopped 'cause it wasn't no *Sports Illustrated* Nigel was looking at in the insides.

He rubbed his jaw and then waved for me to go over and get one, too, and I didn't understand what he meant, where he'd gotten it. He reached up high. He reached up high and handed me one from behind the long, thin cardboard covering all the covers so nobody could really see 'em too good. "This is a good one, I seen this one a couple times before," he said. I flipped to the middle pages and saw in big red letters SIZZLIN' BLACK ON WHITE, and right below them words was a naked black man with an Afro bigger than any I'd ever seen dressed up in some caveman leopard-skin thing going across his chest, all bent down on his knees behind some naked white woman with Dolly Parton blond hair who looked like she was screaming for her life or something, and they were real close, so you could see only a little tiny bit of his weenie and his drooping nuts, and his black hands were groping at one of her blue veiny boobies and she had her own fingers in her mouth, and on the next page another lady lay beneath them both, kissing the other lady's boobs, with long red fingernails grabbing that white lady's private spot, where the black man was already there with his other hand, looking like he was all grabbing and twisting down there in her private parts. All of them were making strange faces like it all hurt real, real bad. It reminded me of things I didn't like to think. I turned a few more pages and some other woman was all in leather with only her face and her boobies showing and a little sliver of her private part hanging out a little tiny opening. She had a whip like the one they used on the horse at the Y camp and had both the feet and the hands of some naked white man in police handcuffs, cuffed to the four poles, spread across some bed, her all smiling holding up a little key in two of her fingers with the longest curling golden fingernails, and on the next page she had whipped the man, 'cause you could see the red welts on his chest, and she was grinning and his weenie was standing straight up and I looked over at Nigel, who was smiling big now, grabbing for some other magazines, saying, "Whoa, this is it," and I turned another page and there was a Chinese nurse like the one who'd helped me to get the X rays on my teeth at Dr. Solomon's last month before, but this one had a little pointy triangle white hat and was naked on the bottom with her legs spread real wide, straddling the top of some metal hospital bed rail, grabbing her own boobie, and on the next page the Chinese lady with the hat was pissing like I never seen a woman do on some white man all bandaged up, and then on the next page, to get her back or something, he'd put all of his hand and part of his arm all the way up and in. "I see you boys are interested in something you know good and well you not old enough to be looking at," and I looked up. Nigel let his thick magazine go down to his side and the creamy fat man was standing halfway down the aisle. "Don't worry, nobody'll know 'sides us three," smiling at us, and all I wanted to do was run.

"If you boys really want to see something nice, I can show you something in the back I save only for the special people. Better stuff than what we're allowed to put out here."

"Yeah," Nigel said, "what ya got back there?" and the

fat man started wobbling toward us slow, grinning so I could see his piss-colored teeth. "Somethin' nice, somethin' you boys are gonna really like, lot better than that stuff there ya lookin' at," and he pulled out a whole bunch of keys on a round metal key chain loop and started jingling and shaking them keys and spinning them around on his finger, shuffling his feet slow at us. "What kind ya got?" Nigel asked, and the fat man smiled and I started moving with my back against the wall, sliding down slow, slow, slow, so I couldn't see the fat man no more but only the light coming from the front door down the next aisle over. I looked at the side of Nigel's face and all I wanted to do was run. Nigel was smiling big and I could hear those keys jingling louder and "Where that little one get to?" and Nigel looked over at me with big eyes, smiling, whispering, "Just like Charles," and I bowed my head and "Ready, Maceo, ya ready?" and I looked up and over and Nigel was stuffing the magazine covered with the *Sports Illustrated* into the back of his swim trunks so they were secure but sticking up a little, then he passed me my stuffed one I had put on the floor, and "Hey, hey," I heard the fat man's voice, "What's this, hey," and "Go, go, go," Nigel whispered fast and easy, and he took off quick down my aisle and out of the store and I heard the fat black man screaming, "What the—what the—you come the fuck back," and saw him wobble out the front of the dirty store, yelling, yelling, chasing Nigel, and I ran down the long aisle and stopped for a moment in front of the glass counter and whirling fans and Yankees game and colored marbles and music and looked quick outside and nothing and I emptied the stuffed *Sports Illustrated* back down onto the floor and saw the fat man's Polaroid sitting on the counter alone and I grabbed it by its straps and took off out the open front as fast as I could right behind them, holding the *Sports Illustrated* Nigel had passed me rolled up in my one hand like that baton them Olympic track guys use on the TV and the Polaroid wrapped around my other hand, the strap jumping around a little loose, hitting my arm as I ran, following slowly on the other side of the street so as to make sure nobody could turn around and grab me easy like those men will do, but close enough so I could see where Nigel was running off to.

The fat owner didn't go very far or very fast and Nigel didn't run his fastest either, just to make sure he wore the fat man out, turning and stopping from time to time, calling him names that made the fat man try and run harder, with his arms pumping up like those Olympic sprinters do on TV, but he'd go only ten feet like that and he'd slow down. After a while the big man stopped, panting, his dark blue shirt wet all the way through with sweat, so it now looked nearly black all over except in a few spots. He put his hands on his knees, stooping over a little like those long-distance runners do on TV when they're all finished. He turned and cursed and shouted at some white lady passing by, "Can you believe these fuckin' little nigger kids these days? Fuckin' delinquents. Fuckin' thieves!" and the white lady quickly crossed the street, and then, out of breath, the fat black man took deep breaths with his cheeks all puffed like those pictures my daddy shows me of Dizzy Gillespie and he did that for a little and then looked across the street and saw me staring at him. "Little fuckin' niggers. Thieves," he said loud so I could hear it, smiling at me. "Fuck you, ya fatso," I said, and I unstrapped his camera and twirled it like a helicopter blade above my head and swung it hard down low like a Reggie Jackson swing against some black fire hydrant. I let the mess fall to the sidewalk. The fat man's milky blue eyes went small and "Nigger," he said loud, jerking his roly body like he was gonna come run over across the street, and I started to run a little and then he stopped and laughed and turned and started waddling back toward his empty newspaper shop, now and then making sure to look back to be certain nobody was coming up from behind him.

Down on the bottom stairs of the Forty-second Street station Nigel was wet all over and his swim trunks dripped sweat slowly off a few edges, making three or four small pools down near close around his white-and-blue Zips he wore without socks. He looked at me coming down the stairs and smiled. He waved the thick *Sports Illustrated* and started doing the original war victory two-step like he'd shown me when he won the first game up by the car with my father. "Huh, no dance for you?" he said, smiling. "Ummm, let's see what you got, got a good one?" And I showed him my empty *Sports Illustrated*. "What happened? What you do with yours?" he asked, and I looked to the ground. "You didn't take any at all?" And I felt the dirty air coming up hot through the subway tunnel, sticking all on me, smelled the nasty stink of some of the open garbage cans that still hadn't been changed, looked at a big fat rat going over the edge of the subway platform to the tracks below, felt hot all over. "You're such a fuckin' baby sometimes, I don't know why in hell I let you hang 'round me. Goddamn sucker, and you said you liked girls, and here are real naked ladies much better than that fat hooker we saw this morning and look what you do . . . ," his voice trailing away from me standing by myself on the bottom stair of the station. "A goddamn faggot is what you are," he said, turning again at me, rubbing his jaw and then smiling at the guy in the token booth, handing him a dollar, buying one token for himself and keeping my fifty cents' change.

NOVO TIEMPO

HE SLIPS IN WITH THE SUN BLEEDING THROUGH THE door and she looks up with everyone else for the burst of afternoon heat. His face in that light. Sun on sweat. His shadow hovering on her. His all-white clothes baggy and swallowing him as my mouth goes back to twisting me into everything my eighteen-year-old Carioca dreams an American man to be. He moves his shadow over our bottles, onto me, off our table, darkening into nothing on the dark floor as the bartender shakes her head *no* at his pleading. He rubs his knuckles. Looks around. Drifts to the bathroom, to the door, to the bar, to the bathroom, to the door, to the bar. He's sweating everywhere and everybody can see. He's rubbing his hands and everybody's frowning. In Portugal's Portuguese he's saying something and the bartender shakes her head no as an orange cat creeps between his legs. My Brazilian girl's beautiful back, breasts, no bra, nipples poking out into a shaft of light, and I dream of her mouth moaning under me as he's mumbling things soft, now loud, loud, making me want to turn my head to see what's coming next but her eyes. The bartender steps back when he steps forward, putting his leg and bare foot on the silver bar, and sliding chairs and grabbing hands and the many men around him, over him, on him hard as his jerks and shrieks fill all of the little bar. One of them gets him in the face and then there's no more sound. Blood drops falling behind the shouts and shuffling shoes rustling his peaceful body through the light with their cool shadows off the floor moving over me, over our bottles with his busted face oozing red but somehow half smiling. A river of red down his white shirt. Another opens the door to that burst of heat with the others rocking, on three throwing him high and headfirst into the wind like he just might fly away, only to bounce, scrape, and scream across the sidewalk. He rolls over, moans, sits on the curb, head in his hands, he cries. They turn and laugh to free Brahma beer along the silver bar. My Brazilian girl's hand through my hair, her moaning mouth in my mind, and "Coca," she says, shaking her head. "Crackhead," she says softly.

THE FIRST THING SMOKING

"IF THROUGH THE LORD'S MERCY HE CAN STILL LOVE and forgive you," my great-aunt Inola Watson said, drawing me close to her white wicker chair and smacking me hard across the nose. "To church," she said. "Preacher Porter'll know what to do," she said, crunching on a piece of ice, and "It's haircut day," I said, "and I'm Jewish now," I said, "and I'll sweat more out in the heat," I said, feeling hot already in my Incredible Hulk underwear, 'cause all this was stupid Preacher Porter's idea in the first place, and "A Jew," she said, "Lord, a Jew, he says," and my eyes began to water but I knew better than to let it come, 'cause she might think it was sweat.

The ceiling fan moved the country air slow around her screened-in porch and I rubbed my face with the hand she didn't have. She had these big, heavy hands, the kind you couldn't wiggle away from easy, and when she hit you in the face, it hurt down around your toes. She touched my nose, my forehead, and looked at her fingers and "Satan," soft, "Satan," screaming, wiping her fingers on her long black dress, sorta half rising up off her chair, hollering "Spirit be gone" in her high, achy voice and I smiled like I could never help 'cause spooks and spirits were the kind of things the kooks said on *Scooby Doo*, not the sorta thing you heard flying out of your great-aunt's mouth, so when I closed my eyes and let out a full giggle, she hit me twice as hard for the sweating and smiling, knocking me clean off my chair with my feet going everywhere, kicking the big bucket of ice over so it clanged with cubes and cold water, and the rest of me slipping across the wood-planked floor. I jumped up quick with my green underwear wet, with the cool water dripping off my knees, jumped quick trying to jerk swing my arm loose but she had me tight again by the arm and when Great-aunt Inola had you like that, there was no getting away.

In the sunlight sneaking across the porch the melting ice and water started to disappear into the worn wood, making the light parts dark. I rubbed my face with the hand she didn't have and thought of screaming and crying, maybe even saying "Stop" real nice with "please," but I already knew that sorta thing didn't do nothing out here in the middle of nowhere with just a cemetery, her, and me and some kooky god only she could see and hear and talk to.

She leaned down, picked up ice cubes, then pushed the big metal wash bucket back over right, now pointing and watching me close to make sure I was gonna do everything just like she'd said. The ceiling fan creaked, moving the air that smelled like cut grass and hot horse shit from Big Head Dwight on Maple and, too, the little fertilizer Great-aunt Inola was able to spread all over her big garden. She had her white wicker chair and one of those foldout metal church chairs she was making me sit on right below the slow fan in order for us to stay cool and keep the devil away. It was hot anywhere else, so I dipped my fingers slow through the ice till they touched the freezing metal bottom. She nodded her head. Took it out and then with her blue-green church fan painted like a peacock's feathers, waved myself slow for the breeze. She sorta smiled. Dropped a big ice cube down my Incredible Hulk Underoos and she nodded. Set my bare feet on the wet wood where the ice cubes had just melted so the cool was on the bottom of my feet. You could feel the wet grooves in the grain there but she shook her head no so I stopped. She looked down and then here and there and not moving for a long while, staring, not hearing me nor nothing else in this world, like she maybe left something or lost something or was looking to say something to the tiny little devils and demons she all the time was saying were pouring in from under the floor. I don't know. I do know I put my feet back on the wet wood while she looked and looked at the somethings I couldn't see, 'cause whatever kept the sweat from coming even a little was what I knew I had to do to keep from getting hot.

"Your feet, boy!" with one hand sweeping me back and up onto the chair so my feet hardly touched the floor again.

"Need to see the preacher is what we need," she said, looking a hundred thousand years old with her shoulders all shlumped down and over. Chewing her ice cubes and loosening her grip on my wrist, with the screen shadows and bugs, just the bugs and bees and creek and the sometimes whistle blows of the train making sounds, with her crunching away on cube after cube, and then, "Need to learn how to act right. Devil or no devil," leaning down and the sizzling sound hurting before the switch bit you, welts and blood growing up and down me as I jumped and danced and hollered like a sissy as Inola stopped with her favorite switch to say "See you" to nobody. "Don't mistake my being old for someone who can't still see, 'cause you ain't that clever, Demon," I guess she was now saying to Lucifer, and though everything was still stinging pretty good, I covered my face and tried not to smile 'cause it was all of it just about to start.

"It's hot," I said, "it's real hot," I said, "and it's not stopping," I said, "what he says ain't working," and she was getting angry how she would, now reaching for the heavy switch again, "and I don't know," I said, " 'cause Uncle Midas said today was my haircut day and he wasn't joking," I said, and what "he wasn't joking" meant was he'd beat your ass worse than anything anywhere and call it a lesson well worth learning if you didn't do exactly what he told you. Like last week after I beat him in checkers right there in his barbershop on a metal chair he'd pulled up below his horse and rodeo trophies he had behind some polished glass like for first-place blue ribbons at school. I beat him bad this time. Normally he'd win. Beat me bad. Tell me not to quit so quick. Use my head. Think. I got tired of losing. And this time I beat him good by employing the tricky cheating ways my pop had taught me how to use only when I really had to win. All my Blackford cousins there in Meadville, all of them were over our shoulders watching, nudging one another, getting excited, smiling, and looking everywhere but at me or Great-uncle Midas, who was the size of Andre the Giant with big Popeye the Sailor arms he'd told us came from his days of breaking horses and knocking spikes through railroad iron. After a few games of this, with me shaking my head, giggling, asking him if he was sure about this move and sure about that move, and then the last game where Great-uncle Midas wouldn't even finish, I started feeling good and big and smart like dead Nigel. Great-uncle Midas along with all the rest of my hovering cousins might see I could do some things all right no matter what size I was, no matter what I looked like, until Midas just stood up.

"What's givin' the little New York slickster some games. Even if he *is* cheatin' me," him there trying to fight back those frowns grown-ups get.

"And y'all think that's cute, huh," he said to everybody, with nobody answering. "And y'all saw him cheat me," and he went and switched on the radio to the Pirates game, so the announcers were just there laughing and talking, filling up all our quiet as he looked hard at each and every one of us. "Funny," he said to them, looking down at the floor.

"Army cuts," Midas then said back and over on Petie, who'd been watching from the barber chair with his Dr. J hair puffed just perfect. That white cape swung around, clipped snug behind the neck before you could say boo, Midas slicing through Petie's big hair real bad, Great-uncle Midas frown-smiling and sweat-boiling in the AC cool, and you could tell everyone in there was getting real uncomfortable watching him bump the barber chair hard with his hip, with those sharp scissors flaring and flashing in and out of Petie's big, lumpy 'fro. My other cousins shifting around in those hard metal chairs, hoping not to be called next for a cut, Midas feeling how he was now, not paying any real attention, with that frown-smile and those scissors going everywhere, drinking, everyone getting to worrying how long it might last, him being like this, and if it'd get worse and most important what it might mean for ass whoopings. So when my little cousin Skamper from Detroit, who doesn't have any sense, didn't know any better than to help himself from sorta giggling with the situation when Uncle Midas asked him to tell the truth if he'd known all along I'd been cheating, Skamper just giggled, tickled, I guess. And Great-uncle Midas just switched off the radio, stopped talking, stopped clipping, looked at Skamper over in the corner facing the wall giggling good with his knees trembling, trying to stuff his whole fist in his mouth to stop it.

"Turn 'round," Midas said. "It's all right, son," he said nice.

And Skamper actually did it.

Midas switched the Pirates back on and went back to clipping and clipping, calm and easy so the veins in his forehead had just about vanished back into his head, hoping to try and sucker someone else into believing he wasn't so mad as he was just before. But my older cousin Salty from Pittsburgh, who'd been around more than anybody, looked at Skamper and shook his head like how Great-uncle Midas might shake his head, so you knew.

I didn't know any better either 'cause I never listened to nobody telling me to lose on purpose, 'cause nobody there was allowed to touch me, so said my pop to all of them, even though all my cousins had warned me that it didn't make no difference what my pop said. That and how I should be smart and not make trouble, to lose if I thought I might win, not to talk big, selling wolf tickets on how smart I was like I might do in some New York City game to some kid my own age. Even Cousin Dwight, who was the size of a fourteen-year-old but my age of exactly eleven to the day and for some sorta reason was supposed to hate me for that and really did, even he had said to go ahead and win and see what happened with a nod and a grin, walking up Midas's steps, so I knew. But to lose. On purpose. Only person I knew who might do such a thing was Big Head himself, 'cause his daddy down in Ebony used to beat him silly over nothing, so he had permanent deep brown scars all over his legs and back and so had gotten real good and accustomed to pleasing folks no matter. But I wasn't Big Head.

Anyways, that day as we all were going out the glass swing door, on down the steps of the house-shop, my great-uncle Midas grabbed me under my underarm and lifted me up with a jerk so my feet dangled high off the ground, and told me to come back alone next week at this very exact time to get the mess called my haircut. And he said, "I don't care who said what, 'cause you need to learn somethin' about standin' up for yourself, talkin' big and cheatin' and then lyin' to a man you're lookin' square in the eye." Looking at my welts and bruises, "And I don't care if you've gotta belt that woman across the face to get here, neither. You know what's right, boy." He let me go and then told Cousin Skamper, who if he'd had any sense would've been the first person out the door, Great-uncle Midas saw Skamper and told him to hold on just one more minute 'cause he wanted to show him how to do something on Maple out back by the stables. No-sense Skamper smiled big at us cousins on the lawn like he'd forgotten everything.

My much bigger older cousins turned and started walking down the hill, slow and smiling, and I said, "He thinks he's going to see Rudolph the Red-Nosed Reindeer," but they looked at me funny, like I was stupid. Junior looked at me, shaking his head like Great-uncle Midas might shake his head, and said, "Runt," he said, smiling at me, "remember, runt. A hard head makes a soft behind," and my cousin Mac said, "Won't be smiling long," and Cousin Mesley said, "I ain't never seen the man lose at nothin'," and older cousin Brian said, "Ain't nothing good to learn back there on that big black mare," and Mac said louder to himself, "Forget that giggling, too," and little Cousin Brian said, "He ain't got no soft, big house Watson hands, neither," looking at me, and Cousin Salty said, "Never forget any lesson and you might get a few less," and Cousin Petie with the half-cut, unfinished, messed-up head, who was named after my pop's middle name and so for some reason liked me a little more than those other ones even though I was lighter and a Watson, Cousin Petie with the messed-up 'fro said, "Ya better thank Skamper for giggling." And then Big Head Dwight went, "Skamper don't stand a chance."

'Cause my cousins were sent there summers and now me, too, to learn something from Great-uncle Midas and most already knew his belief on teaching you in the quickest way possible the right way to be a Blackford, which a lot of times meant lessons. The days were his, my pop had said, so I could be with my other cousins. And the nights, Inola's. But Inola didn't always let me go, making me sit with stupid Preacher Porter with his snow-white suit and white cowboy hat, all of us in there all hot and sweating, them doing their Jesus pray things to me inside that trailer they called their church in the middle of nowhere with posters of Jesus as a black man taped on the walls with those nasty fluorescent lights on me like they have at school.

So anyways, you could hear the horses making their sounds, smell them everywhere you looked, and before we got to the bottom of Great-uncle Midas's little hill, the glass door opened and a little brown hand and the glass door slamming and in a moment like that Cousin Skamper screaming long and hard for his life, which made all of my cousins stop and turn and sit a little closer to the door to hear Great-uncle Midas grunting and Skamper whining, "Nooooo," and yipping, "Ahhhh," from the long stables behind the small red house with everybody all of us going, "Ohhhhhhhhh," at some of the real loud grunts and snaps and screams making me good and scared, 'cause though nobody was allowed to get me, Inola and that preacher were already doing it and I knew there was nobody around anywhere who could save me, and "Huh, boy?" Great-aunt Inola said in the heat.

And I was about to tell her how I'd turned Jewish just this very day. And all about the sweating, which was most certainly allowed in that religion, 'cause I'd seen my Jewish friends at school sweat like crazy in front of everybody without any sorta whoopings, slaps, or switchings. I was gonna tell her how she could just leave me be and I'd be all right 'cause I didn't even think Jewish people had a hell to speak of, nor any folks named Satan or Lucifer or Jesus you had to be protected from, but she was eyeing me hard how she sometimes did when she wasn't sure if she should go for her switch or something worse, so I kept quiet with that stuff.

She had car-tire-black-colored skin that made my ma wonder out loud back in New York, right after my ma's grandma died, where my pop's aunt Inola truly came from, no matter how my pop's face twisted up, screaming,

"You can't say that." Car-tire black was darker than any Watson or Blackford anywhere on Earth, save maybe one day me if I was out in the sun forever for the rest of my life, but there was my ma to account for some of that, which all my cousins here in Meadville, Pennsylvania, seemed to point out to me first thing before they'd even said hello.

Great-aunt Inola didn't like my ma and called her black bitch. Said so 'cause I was a Watson and look how dark I was becoming and that couldn't be her blood doing that. And then how I should stay inside out of the sun and how there weren't that many Watson men in my generation, and what would happen to our family if things kept going dark and down like this? "At this rate you'll have to go off and marry some white girl just to make it tolerable again," with her nice voice, smiling at me as I looked at the backs of my hands, much lighter than hers, and "Your father, Franklin, shoulda gone and found a nice girl," she'd say, "his pick of anyone," she'd say, "and look what he does, Lord," she'd say, "a nice girl, more suitable to our class and color," which didn't make any kind of sense looking at her there, dark, and thinking of my ma, who gave me things with smiles and caresses and was the color of coffee with lots of milk in it.

You could already tell what she thought about me but maybe her god or that Preacher Porter said different, 'cause when she kept me, she beat on me at least twice, three times a day with those switches, sizzling through the air like frying bacon, wrapping around my legs stinging hot, all the while her saying how both she and God loved me, and how even though I was dark, I was her favorite, was why she was working so hard through God's hands to save me with her hard voice when her eyes were big and I was sprawled, out of screams, not moving, all over the floor and she was sitting awhile herself 'cause she'd gotten tired. And, too, with her soft voice when she was tucking the blankets too tight, up on my throat under my chin, with them overstarched blankets pinning me to the bed, before saying, "That Franklin," soft and easy to herself, as if my pop would hear her while she turned all the lights off and closed my door, making the whole world dark so the walls could start their whisperings, and the things coming out from under the floor, and I'd try not to grit my teeth hard like I would to make it all stop but I'd get to grinding them anyway, so I'd have to be careful not to wake her up next door. I'd wait awhile with the sheets pulled all the way over my head and keep still as could be for as long as I could, listening to the whispering walls and big things crawling around the ceiling, and after a while I'd get up and run over and turn all the lights back on and hope I could get to sleep and back up early before she got up, so she wouldn't be so mad come next day for the lights being on.

'Cause I guess I wasn't doing so well as I was supposed to since me and Chris Clipper watched Nigel get sliced up in the belly by the side of the doughnut shop. Nigel falling over onto the sidewalk, bleeding all over his Thurman Munson Yankees pin-striped shirt and beige shorts and legs, dark blood all over everywhere on the sidewalk, trying to hold his guts in with his hand. Not talking so big anymore about "no fool ever taking his hard-earned money," which he'd really taken from me, as stuff came rolling out of moaning Nigel, him asking for help and his mama as we just watched and watched him there 'cause he would talk big and do things to you. Do things like steal your money and tell lies to get you in trouble and for no good reason you could ever figure punch you in the mouth 'cause he was older and bigger and knew you couldn't do nothing about it. So we watched him moan as stuff eased out of him. He'd done a lot of bad things, Nigel with his big mouth, bullying people all around, though after he was dead and the way his mama was upset and how waxy plastic he looked lying there at the funeral my ma made me go to, nobody seemed to feel any better, him having finally gotten in the gut what we all hoped, thought, and prayed at one time or another he'd one day get. So everybody tried to smile more and kinda stopped altogether talking about the things he'd do to you for no good reason and made up sweet stories and full-blown lies to tell his mama to make her feel better about her awful Nigel. And as punishment for watching and kinda smiling some when Nigel got it good, later that day when I got home, my ma's grandma died. My great-grandma who'd taken care of me some. And now I wasn't doing so well with the nightly nightmares that came on me soon as I closed my eyes for even just a moment.

The rest of the Watsons, like my pop, looked mostly white and a lot of them could pass that way when they wanted to be something else, like some of them, my ma said, had already gone and done to disappear into who knows who, she'd said, frying me sausages, putting orange juice in my Cap'n Crunch just the way I liked, with car horns and bus engines creeping from down below into our kitchen. They'd owned a plantation down south once and my grandpa Maceo and great-uncle Midas had lived and worked hard as slaves for the Watsons on that very same land. Great-uncle Midas hated the Watsons for that. And even more when his brother married my grandma and changed his name from Blackford to Watson, 'cause for those people, Lord only knows why, my ma said, a name means everything. "And do you still want to go? You're big enough to choose, you know, because that family owned . . ." but she didn't finish, just looking out the window down at the cars below. I looked at her 'cause I didn't know all of it exactly what she meant.

"There was a time," she said, "when some rich black families didn't want to be black and sometimes treated other black families worse than even white people, and part of your father's family was once a family like that," she said. "You can come and send your great-grandmother off right if you want to, if you feel like you're a big enough boy," she said. "Maybe it'll make your bad dreams disappear forever, Maceo," she said when my pop wasn't around to help me decide. He thought I was too young for death up close. He didn't know all of it about Nigel.

I didn't go.

Great-aunt Inola also had sky-blue eyes, behind silver winged glasses and beautiful, silky silver hair that seemed to glow soft blue when the sun came through the porch and hit it right. Long, straight hair going all the way down her back like my grandma had, like a black Cherokee Indian from the movies, like Inola'd never cut it ever in all her natural-born life. Soft so it blew all over with the lightest breeze and she'd have to grab to hold it, fumbling with both her hands, smiling with her face calm in a way that made you want to get close to her long hair and let it blow around your face. When it was like that, I could almost see how my dad could've loved her so much. She stood tall for a Watson and had a big silver cross hanging on a linked silver chain that swung back and forth across her belly when she moved here or there or jerked quick to hit me hard with one of those big, stony hands.

That summer my own hair seemed to be slowly twirling from soft mixed curls to tight black kinks and in the last weeks with Midas, in that hot summer sun, my skin was changing, too, getting darker and darker like they couldn't believe. My hair was big, soft, and poofy and everyone still liked to touch the top of it, especially the white people at my school back in New York. All my older relatives on both sides, Blackford and Watson, would pull me over by the arm to touch my hair, too. People liked it. They'd do that and pull my short-sleeved shirt up, not believing the tan lines of my skin, trying to figure for themselves which way I was gonna turn.

I had Watson for a last name but they weren't too sure 'cause my grandma Georgia Watson was a light, light Watson with some red Cherokee Indian in her face and my grandpa Maceo Blackford was a dark-as-night Blackford who'd gotten scorched working most of his life out in the sun on black Great-aunt Inola's and Great-grandma Pocahontas the half-red Cherokee's land. And my pop was real, real light with straight hair but mean and tough like a real Blackford, so they thought I had a chance to go either way. Nobody knew how to account for my ma's family for coming out of Flint by way of Marion, Arkansas, so they tried not to count them.

None of it made any kind of sense to me no matter how I tried to sit down and put it together.

Everyone else seemed to know, though.

I was staying up the way with my great-aunt Inola, a

woman, a Watson, a bad thing, me the only one with a woman, which my cousins laughed and laughed about, while Big Head Dwight and older cousin Brian were down the way with my great-uncle Midas Blackford closer to town. Those two were his favorites. All the rest of everybody was spread everywhere far. All of us cousins wanting to be down with Great-uncle Midas 'cause he was near town and let you do things and didn't make you go to church and had air-conditioning in every room and real Arabian horses from Arabia and sometimes, if you were in his favor, he might take you out for a ride, leave everyone else behind, go wherever you might want to go, Great-uncle Midas showing you things to look at in the mountains, in the trees, at the clouds in the sky. Riding slow with the horses' heads let go, Midas telling you tall tales and legends and things you might want to know about the creeks and streams and the Indian tribes that once ruled all the lands around here.

But only Big Head Dwight and older cousin Brian were staying with him. And only Big Head Dwight was allowed to go riding alone. All tall through town, everyone on the trains, walking around town, stopping to look at him on any one of those big fine horses during the day and even all through the night, galloping with the breeze through the waving fields, smiling down along the creek, mostly, these days, on Great-uncle Midas's favorite, Maple. Big Head with his slingshot or bow and arrows like a real full-blooded Indian, going without a saddle sometimes in the hot sun, even making it all the way out by Inola and me with his face painted red and blue like an Indian. Standing up doing circus pony tricks like it was nothing, going

"Woo, woo, woo" like a real Apache might do on Sunday-afternoon TV. Big Head Dwight smiling and then moving giant Maple to step all through Inola's garden to shit and piss. Then rearing Maple up on two legs like the Lone Ranger does on Silver, me trying to shake Inola out of from wherever she was into some sorta sense so she could see it was Big Head Dwight doing it like I'd been saying all along and not some giant devil demon with hooves I brought along to Meadville from New York. Big Head on those big horses without a worry in the world, my cousin, my age, looking and laughing and pointing at me, knowing I was gonna get it real bad, and soon inside on that screened-in porch me under that slow fan all hot and bursting with heat, trying like crazy to wipe the sweat off everywhere to hide it before she came to. Him giggling at me sticking my feet and hands and head into the cooling bucket, with Inola still holding me good and tight while not seeing anything, Inola looking off at who knows what, mumbling not English words to I don't know who.

And when Great-uncle Midas was clipping hair and got to dipping into his gold-plated flask with MIDAS TOUCH on the side, he'd say things all over in front of everybody, like how my daddy had gone off and married some light nigger-honky of a woman who'd gone and turned him into a natural-born pussy, 'cause my pop didn't even carry his gun no more. With Big Head Dwight there always making faces, laughing the loudest at just about anything Midas said about me. And how they were raising me up like I was a little pansy white girl, which was why I was gonna grow up into a nigger faggot of the worst degree, hating my own of my own color, going around chasing high yella girls with good hair and even one day trying for dem New York City blondes that go goo over some wanting-to-be-high-class, big-house, sharp-ass city nigger.

"I seen it all," he'd say, clipping.

"I watched your daddy," he'd say, picking.

"And your mama, too," putting white powder on a neck.

"But I plan to have you understand.

"To stand up for yourself. To be a man," looking at all of us in the face, and "Look how much Maceo lets that woman beat on him," as they all looked at me there trying to hide the many big red welts on my legs, face, and arms.

And with one of his cigars alone and smoking, getting big and ashy on the ashtray, he'd be drinking, really getting going glaring at me, clipping fast, bumping the chair hard around with his hip, eyeing that checkerboard on the shelf, eyeing me, saying to all my cousins' smiles, "Maceo ain't all to blame, though, but that Petie"—which is what he called my pop—"and that wanna-be whitey"—which is what he called my ma—"gotta own up to this," as Midas stopped clipping and shook his head, which sometimes made me feel better, it not being all my fault. But not really better. The better like when your whooping gets put off till after dinner. "Bet you cry a lot, huh, boy, huh," he'd say. "That Watson bitch hits ya and I bet ya bawl, don't ya, boy," he'd say with all my cousins grinning, hoping to see something worth seeing, like someone getting beaten silly with a belt or a good heavy switch while he jumped and screamed like a little sissy bitch trying his everything to shake an arm loose, which, if you weren't next, was maybe the funniest thing in the whole wide world to see.

Great-uncle Midas would go to town, to the general

store, smile, and buy them things Great-aunt Inola would never think to get me. On shopping day sometimes we'd see them and be there standing around in the store, her and him hating each other and then me and Big Head 'cause Dwight was always following Great-uncle Midas all around calling him Big Daddy, holding Midas's cigars and such things. And those two old folks would be there just talking long and fake nice about nothing, with Midas spitting nasty brown chew spit inside the store as she talked and it'd be getting her, so she'd be shifting her weight from one foot to the other in that heat with her shiny black shoes and starched long dress, talking sorta down at him with that soft, silky voice of hers, him in red suspenders with his old railroad shirt untucked around the sides with sweat marks way down under his arms, all down deep the front of his chest, smelling like he'd been working outside in the stables in the hot heat for a long time, his arms bulging and glistening and I know she'd want to belt him for it. Belt him 'cause she knew he knew I was supposed to be with him, belt him 'cause he knew the things she was trying to do to me and was telling me to make her stop. But nobody'd, neither one of them, say nothing about nothing 'cause I guess he was who he was and she thought sure Lucifer would come and take care of it soon enough. Cast him straight to the fiery gates of hell, where every last one of us was gonna go unless Preacher Porter got ahold of you long enough to get his truth of God in you, but I knew there was no hope for him 'cause of what Inola said. And no hope for me neither 'cause when I closed my eyes, trying to remember all the things that Preacher said to do and not to do, all I saw were blue-eyed ghosts burning and screaming while getting stabbed, so they fell over with all their guts and blood falling out of their bellies and mouths, which was why I was thinking to maybe become a Jew so their God might stop Inola and Preacher from hitting me and let the things that happened with dead Nigel slide and let me sleep some without the dreams, which wouldn't go away.

Standing there all bored, with the store smelling of oak and pine and oil and horses, with Big Head grinning big about who knows what, you'd get so you'd wanna wheel around and kick something over 'cause she'd have garden seeds and cabbage and bubbles and her stupid gettin'-the-devil-out-ya Preacher Porter potion things like that for me, and Great-uncle Midas'd have good things like horse hay and footballs and fishing poles and slingshots and BB guns and *Playboys*. He'd just sorta shake his head at me as Inola took me out by the hand, 'cause I wasn't doing nothing about what she was doing, which was nobody's fault but my own, Midas said. Then she'd take me past the preacher's, where they'd have me strip down to my underwear and he'd close his eyes and touch my forehead, chanting this and that prayer over me, pouring smelly things over my head, and then tell her things to try to do to me. She'd take me back to her house, where in the heat in my underwear again for a long time she'd hold me by the arm and then like that grab me close and switch me.

So I tried not to think those things and I tried not to move but I'd get sweating anyway and I knew she and that preacher were getting ready for something bad. She had her suitcase packed and mine, too. So I dipped my hand in the ice bucket again but nothing happened. No cooler. It was hot and the sweat was coming. Under the slow fan she began to drift into her stare as I tried to get the sweat off my nose quick while she was looking out across the heat snaking off the thin road, over the fields and fields of tall green grass, across the creek whose sounds you could make out from here, past the rows and rows of big weeping willow trees, to the faraway puke-yellow farmhouse on the hill Great-aunt Inola said was huge but looked small from here. Dark green and blue mountains were past that, fanning out behind the little yellow house like a peacock's tail or Great-aunt Inola's church fan. Great-uncle Midas, who was gonna cut my hair in an hour, I didn't care how, lived near those dark green mountains and yellow house with his beautiful Arabian horses on the other side of the two streets and rail station, which was town. Looking at her there staring, I couldn't put her together with the lady my pop loved to talk on and on about being the nicest aunt on Earth. The only one who never hit nobody and who'd talk people out of whooping your hide. What with her praying and crossing herself like my ma did on her knees when her grandma died, but different. Mean and nasty with it, like she was trying to figure out a way to get ya. Sometimes I thought there was something wrong with her, too, and then when it was like that, it didn't hurt half so bad when she really got going. But I didn't think that too much. Only sometimes when I thought about my ma on her knees in our kitchen praying and crying after she got off the phone with her sister and wouldn't stop for whatever reason.

After we dropped my ma off at the Newark airport that next day, that morning we left, I asked my dad about the Grandpa Maceo and Great-uncle Midas slave thing, and "No," he said, "no, no," he said, "who told you that?" he said. "Your mother tell you that," with his face going tight and I knew I'd said something I shouldn't have said with the way my pop didn't say anything but looked forward. Quiet with both his hands gripping on the steering wheel, with his teeth clenched and his jaw and his tight face he got sometimes when maybe he wanted to grab a waiter who wouldn't wait on us 'cause we were black, or like the fried-oysters guy in Martha's Vineyard my pop grabbed around the throat, wanting to kill him for calling my ma a stupid nigger or a jungle bunny or a spear chucker or something like that. Driving in the quiet, he had his face like that. My pop went for a long time, no radio on, quiet with the tight face, and then leaned forward and looked up and pulled the Cadillac over and looked at me and put the top down, which he never did 'cause the black car was a classic and my ma didn't like the top down on account of the wind in her hair. He fake smiled the way they were doing a lot since Nigel but didn't say anything, and there were clouds but like they were listening to him, watching us, 'cause they wrenched back, all of them, like they were blinds my pop had on an invisible string. Them clouds wrenched back and blew away, and like that our summertime was right full with summer heat and on all the chrome the sun exploding in a thousand different ways, in your eyes to make you squint but smile, how I guess you might want it with the top down with the wind and the sun and the heat everywhere, so I closed my eyes, sweating for a while, feeling good, moving fast through the hot, wet air, with the bright chrome and my dad's puff of white hair blowing back with the wind. And me starting to feel not so heavy but good again in a way I hadn't been able to feel for some long time because of the way things had gone with God and Nigel and my great-grandmother and my mother's tears right when she dropped the phone with a lot of crying, trying to convince us how Great-grandma had really had a real full life.

I woke up to kid screams and the rattle-roar of the wooden roller coaster. The heat and the sun and my dad telling me to come on, with his Yankees hat on he only put on when we were going to go out and have a whole lot of fun.

The swing.

The Spider.

The go-carts.

The bumper cars, where my pop talked and talked to the attendant while letting me stand on his toes to be tall enough to drive alone. And then big-belly laughing while letting me line him up from far away to ram him good, so though I could hardly see above the wheel, I could hear him grinning like he hadn't for real since he found out how I just stood and watched Nigel get killed by some not-so-big kid with a knife.

Later on, feeling good and tired, with the night air and the top back up, roaring into the mountains, deep into the night, with a speedometer green glow over my dad's face, he didn't say anything, his face back twisted tight, so I knew he was thinking things he didn't want to say out loud.

"Your granddaddy wasn't a slave," my pop said out of nowhere. "Nor your great-uncle Midas, despite what your mother thinks," he said. "They broke horses for many folks around Ebony. Horses, steers, buffalos, pigs, ducks, dogs, anything, even a camel. Someone had a camel," he said. "Whatever folks were having problems with. Your grandfather met your grandmother and they loved each other and got married and lots of the town folks didn't like it 'cause your grandfather was dark, and 'cause of all the land and money and cotton your grandma's family had, well, people had come to regard them as white, which was why they tolerated our family having so much. And that wasn't allowed then. People didn't like it. A dark person and a white person. Your grandfather Maceo was walking down the street, tall, 'cause that's the man he was, and the folks were of course giving him looks and stares and saying things under their breath there in Ebony, and someone finally came up from behind and pushed him off the sidewalk. And your grandfather, Maceo, being proud and hotheaded like us all, went over with his gun already out to the white man, began pistol-whipping him in the middle of the street. And then when the man wasn't moving anymore but still saying the terrible things he'd been shouting the whole time, your grandfather shot him twice. Once in each knee. The town went crazy and they came that night and burned your grandmother's cotton gin down and a few barns and killed some horses and burned some cotton fields and lynched your great-uncle Cleo and were looking to lynch your granddaddy."

"Lynch?" I said.

"They wanted to hang him by the throat from a tree and kill him," my pop said, and "Oh," I said.

"And he barely escaped. Escaped by sneaking through the woods on his belly, and when the sun came up, he ran and ran as fast as he could and caught the first thing smoking out of town."

I wasn't sure what to make of anything as we roared past red taillights and that eerie light on my dad's face, but he didn't hear me. Just went on, " 'Cause sometimes, even though it's very bad and very wrong, there's nothing you can do but run. There some things you can't beat and there's nothing you can do because some things in this world are just too big and bad to beat and nothing you can do but die or get out of town as quick as possible on the first thing smoking and find some place new and start again in some place better and hope you don't gotta do it again." I didn't know what to say.

"He held on underneath the train out of town and made it up here to work on the railroads, how we came to have to change our name from Blackford to Watson. To become the way-up-north Watsons here in Meadville, Pennsylvania. Your grandma's maiden name," he said with a raise of his hand to the stars like he hadn't said anything at all. Looking straight ahead at the white lines flying at us as we went past the red taillights of the few other cars, my dad's green face frowning big in the speedometer glow with the stars everywhere and the cold now on the passenger window against the top of my head as I looked up at the stars, and no matter how I yawned, my ears wouldn't pop, and "Hold your nose," my pop finally said, "blow." And I did and he touched my hair as we passed some of the last cars, us flying, I'm sure, going the speed of light, my pop without his Yankees hat on, looking at nothing but the straight-ahead dark nothing coming at us fast with that green pained frown across his face, so I wished I'd never asked about anything about me or those people, and for the rest of the while in the car in the quiet like that.

THE AIR COMING THROUGH INOLA'S SCREENED-IN PORCH felt cooler now where the sting of the smack touched my face, my legs and arms burning, but I was sweating now and watching her, too, through the warm screen shadows slinking across her and the metal bucket, toward me. She was looking at me, waiting for me to say something, I guess, back to that Jewish stuff, and it was real stuffy and hot even though that squeaky fan and she was sweating some now, too, on her nose, and I got to thinking about my great-grandma who I'd never see again and how she'd smile at me and never hold my wrists like this, hitting me all the time like this, and I got to wishing my great-aunt Inola were the one dead and buried up in some cemetery somewhere and not my great-grandma in Michigan, and it was getting me so I didn't know what to say or do, making me want to cry 'cause I couldn't see my great-grandma ever again anymore ever not one last time never, and who knows, maybe I was crying some, and "Get your suitcase," she said, "we're going to Preacher's," she said, "it's not safe here," she said. "Boy! That sweat on you," Great-aunt Inola said, staring at my face. I turned and grabbed the wash bucket. Turned back and bashed her with everything I had right in that mouth, making her scream, "Ohhhhh," as she let go of me and fell over hard to the ground with that splash of water and cubes sliding over her face across the floor, and "Lucifer, Lucifer," with that achy voice, with both her hands covering her face. I stood over her and then kicked her in the gut when she went to reach for me. And then kicked her again. And then again. And once with the bucket. And again near her face, making her winged glasses break and twist, flopping up into the air into that ice bucket lying on the floor, making me smile 'cause of that voice of hers moaning how she liked to make me moan, her hair everywhere across the floor, holding her belly, and I looked at her and ran.

I ran.

I ran up the road as she screamed and down the road as she screamed and then across the creek, through the grass, up the hill, into the cemetery where Great-uncle Cleo, Great-aunt Inola's old dead husband, and my grandpa Maceo were buried. From the hill I could still hear her screaming, "Maceo," but it got up to me soft without all the other stuff she always had in her voice when she was screaming up on me close. I watched her looking up and down the street, behind the house, to the garden side, and to the other side, where the switches grew tall and the wet clothes hung. She tore loose a big, big switch and started up my way but stopped. I waved at her. She went back in the house awhile. When she came out, she had on a light blue hat and her long silver hair up tight in a bun with the same long black dress, which covered everything, coming way down past her feet, with the big switch in her swinging hand and a full, big brown grocery bag in the other. I could see her fiddling with her keys, locking the door.

She had on all black and her light blue hat, so when she started moving, she looked like she was floating slow like the ghost in my dreams and then just her light blue hat gliding along the tall green bushes and then there was no seeing her at all. After a while I figured I better make it over to Great-uncle Midas's house.

In my green Hulk underwear I walked down the hill past the house, across the cold creek, through the heat, sweating everywhere while crossing the fields and fields of tall green bushes up around my shoulders, warm mud in between my toes, past the rows and rows of big weeping willows with the sun coming through, making shadows, with the blue mountains getting bigger and bigger, through knee-high purple and orange and pink wildflowers with white butterflies everywhere above them, on past the gigantic yellow house that went on and on, down one of the two streets of town where all the older white and black people looked at me funny, on through to the concrete stairs going up the little hill of my great-uncle Midas's house.

I opened the glass door and wanted to say something, 'cause maybe I could stay here the rest of the time, and Great-uncle Midas didn't even look at me but kept on clip-clipping with scissors on the last of Cousin Petie's hair. The air was on and all my sweat felt cold. There was a wet brown paper shopping bag folded up nice sitting on one of the chairs next to Big Head Dwight, who was smiling at me. I saw it and started sweating all over everywhere like I was right outside running around in that hot country heat even though that cold air was blowing hard.

"Looks like you been running from something," Midas said.

"No, sir," I said.

"In your green underwear like that. Are you sure?" he said.

"Yes, sir," I said.

"What are the four things I hate most, Dwight?"

"Cheaters, liars, quitters, and runners," Dwight said.

"Saw your granddaddy do that once. Maybe it's your name," Midas said. "He shoots a white man dead for no good reason, Dwight, 'cause the white man cursed him about marrying Georgia, maybe something small. And instead of fighting like a man with us, his family, he's gotta go and make a run for it, change his name, leave our brother Cleo to stay and get hanged for nothing. No, I don't much like runners," Midas said quietly, clipping, switching on the Pirates, and I thought I might just fall out right there and play dead or maybe make a run for it right then but I knew I probably wouldn't make it out the door before Midas had his hands on me. Cousin Skamper had tried that his giggling day and had gotten the worst beating of his life and still couldn't sit down right.

Cousin Salty was flipping through a *Playboy*. Little cousin Brian was staring at the floor. Cousin Skamper was standing by the door with his head leaned into the corner facedown 'cause he was still in trouble for trying to run and for screaming like a sissy when he got it. The air conditioner was right above him, dripping stuff so his shirt was wet in a messed-up arrow going down, but he didn't look like he felt a thing. None of them were supposed to be there. Great-uncle Midas pointed and Dwight went inside the house through the blue beaded door-curtain and came back with one of my white tank tops. A pair of shorts. My shoes. He smiled.

Great-uncle Midas pointed at the shirt. I put it on, then my shorts, and though my cousins giggled, he nodded, so I didn't care. "Sit down and put them shoes on, boy, with mud on ya feet," he said, and then, "Ya late, ya know that? And ya all wet with sweat, ya know that? Have ya been runnin' from something, son?" and "No, sir," I said, and Big Head Dwight smiled at me real big, so I could see his teeth. Nobody said anything and you could hear the air conditioner going hard above the door. I sat there. I didn't know what to do. Thought if Great-uncle Midas made a move at me, maybe I'd make a run for it. I watched him. Great-uncle Midas would stop and look at me, then the checkerboard, then keep cutting. My other cousins watched me while trying not to. It wasn't good to look at anybody too close. I looked around; Great-uncle Midas had two shiny chrome and red leather barber chairs that swiveled around and around. He had all the green and blue gels and white powders and clear oils and brushes and combs and picks and paper towels standing next to one another on a small white marble counter with his many clippers and razors on hooks hanging down. There was a big mirror that stretched all the way across the whole porch, so you could always catch some kind of look at the person getting a cut. Salty, with his hair all gone, oohed and aahed and picked up another *Playboy* and looked at me and shook his head and flipped pages and now smiled into the pictures again, oohing and aahing. Nobody had any hair left but me. The room smelled like aftershave and air-conditioning and musks and colognes. Those were the same smells of all the black and brown railroad men that walked down past me by the general store who'd just had a cut. Great-uncle Midas took a big swig out of his gold-plated flask. His eyes were red. Skamper looked down as little cousin Brian stared over at me, then the floor.

"Ya next," Great-uncle Midas shouted.

Cousin Petie got out of the chair, brushing his now bald head with his hand. Bald. "Come here, boy," Great-uncle Midas said again, and Big Head Dwight said, "Go on, boy," and I looked at him 'cause I guess I hated him, too, I

guess I hated them all and wished they were all dead instead of my great-grandma, and I knew I was gonna
dream about them all getting it in the worst way from
devils and demons with flaming swords and sharp, pointed
pitchforks cutting arms and heads off, which made me
jump up screaming in the middle of the night. I'd pull the
blankets up over my head and curl up and get as small
as I could, 'cause out here there wasn't anything between
those dreams and me and sometimes even the big light
didn't do a thing to stop them from coming. It'd been like
that for some while. I knew.

Great-uncle Midas picked me up and plopped me down
hard into one of them kiddie chairs with the silver chrome
arms stretched out on both sides so as to rest on the red
leather arms of the barber chair.

Great-uncle Midas swung the white cape around me
and lassoed it around my neck and I wanted to tell him
something about something, like the dream of him getting
his head cut off and burned crispy by a flaming sword or
him getting pitchforked right in the ass with all manner of
snakes and bug things coming out or how my great-
grandma hovered calm over my bed when I went to sleep,
asking why I did it, so I didn't know what to do, or about
Great-aunt Inola flying around on a broom, trying to
come down to whack me with a big green switch the size
of the Empire State Building, as he crank-crank-cranked
me up so he could get at my head real easy, but none of
that dream stuff would come out my mouth.

He grabbed my chin and jerked my head back and
there was a *snap* and the clippers were on me and my big,
poofy hair was coming down past my eyes in patches and
clumps as I felt the cold, thin blade digging into my scalp,

and "You givin' that woman trouble over there, Maceo?" and "No, sir," I said, and "Ya lyin' ta me, boy?" and "No, sir," I said, and in the mirror Big Head Dwight was smiling as Cousin Petie shook his head as little Cousin Brian shifted some in his seat as Cousin Salty oohed and aahed some more at the pictures as Skamper tried not to be there and Cousin Petie now rubbed his head, and "Why were ya late, boy, ya can't hear right when I speak ta ya?!" Great-uncle Midas said, and I didn't know what to say and he jerked my head down so I was looking at his spit-polished black shoes, and "Ya hear me now, boy," with his big, heavy hand pressing down on my head so my neck hurt real bad as he started on the other half he hadn't even touched yet.

Great-uncle Midas was graying, though he'd lost no hair and had all his teeth despite all the fights my pop said he'd been in. He had big brown eyes that danced and jerked when he'd gotten to his flask early like he had today. You could see them all red going everywhere in the mirror. He rocked my head forward and snapped the clippers and tons of black, cottony hair rolling down my face as I tried to blow it off my nose, outta my eyes, but there was just no use.

"Quit ya fidgetin', boy! 'Cause if that nice lady says ya been actin' up, I'm gonna come on up dere wid my belt and lean inta ya with that leather. Don't matter ta me what ya daddy says 'bout it neither, 'cause I'll still kick his ass if I need ta, 'cause if ya lyin' ta me, no tellin' when or how I'll ever stop, gotta call the National Guard to get me off ya. Try and see if it don't happen!"

And he snapped my head to the right, and thinking on him never stopping and how long it'd take the National

Guard to come and get him off and I just about wished I was dead right then. And there was Big Head Dwight's stupid mouth all smiling and grinning big and wide at me in the big, long mirror at every turn of the chair. When twenty minutes was up, all my hair was gone. Bald. Six shades lighter than the rest of me. Terrible. My older cousin Brian came in and slapped Big Head five as I dusted myself off of hair and Great-uncle Midas smiled at Brian, who wasn't supposed to be there, but he was there and Great-uncle Midas said, "Dwight, you and Maceo go on out front and play till I'm done wid ya cousin," to which they all looked at me, and I at Big Head Dwight smiling real big in the mirror, getting out of his chair.

Everybody called him Big Head Dwight, even little Cousin Brian and Dwight's mama back down in Ebony, 'cause he had this huge head that made you wonder how in the world his little pencil-thin neck could hold it up, but as we were walking out Cousin Salty said, "Hey, Big Head, ya know Maceo's been calling ya Big Head all behind ya back."

Uncle Midas's house was on top of a small grass hill with white speckles sprinkled all about, which must've been fertilizers or grass food or some chemical 'cause it burned and made you itch your skin when you sat in it. There was an old brown football with no air in it with grass growing around it. I went outside down the hill. I picked the football up, wondering why I hadn't ever seen it before and why nobody had ever moved it all this time, even when Big Head had to mow the lawn. I turned it around and it was wet on the bottom where the big dent was and the grass, where it had been, was brown and mushed in good.

I dropped it to the ground and watched it flopping down the hill toward the sidewalk and I turned to say something and I was on the ground and Dwight was screaming, screaming and the grass was wet on the side of my face and I had dirt in my mouth and he was screaming, and he flipped me over and his eyes got really, really big like they were gonna bust out of his skull and he had his knees in my chest and his teeth were out like he was gonna eat me up. He started swinging and caught me in the eye and I covered up, hoping and praying Cousin Petie or someone big would come over and pull this fool offa me, and Stupid hit me on the top of the head and in the ear and the throat, so it was hard to breathe, and Big Head was gasping and my balls and he was squeezing and I screamed and he had his knees in my belly and I moved my arms from my head and he caught me in my lower lip and I was beginning to cry like I knew I shouldn't and he was laughing and then I felt his teeth on my shoulder and there something happened.

It wasn't slow either. Just a snap, like one of Great-uncle Midas's clippers.

It snapped and I screamed and grabbed Big Head Dwight's nuts and rolled left and rocked right and he went rolling down the hill with me squeezing both his nuts with both my hands all the while, now up and punching him in the balls and he was screaming and I jumped up and kicked Big Head Dwight in the face, and I was crying good now and jumped up and landed on Big Head Dwight's chest with both my knees like Superfly Jimmy Snucka and I was screaming, screaming, screaming and I was up and Dwight was holding his nose and I whirled around and kicked him in his ribs and then his face and then his ear and Stupid was curled up now and cursing and I went for his nose again and bit him there and, spitting and spitting, screamed, "Fuck you, Dwight. Fuck you, Big Head jerk," and got to straddling his chest, punching and punching, and punching and punching, my arms moving like a windmill going around and around all about his covered-up head, not caring where the hits landed but only that they hurt real good, and he was crying now hard and I bent down and bit him right like he'd done me on the shoulder and began choking him with two hands all about his thin chicken neck, shaking and shaking him so his head was hitting the grass hard and I wanted that neck to break and his big head to zing off and I slowed 'cause the snap was off and I could see what I was doing.

I got up and grabbed the football, feeling like I wanted to kill him good 'cause I felt terrible all over, with the taste of blood in my mouth, and I smiled and threw that football at the balled-up, moaning, crying, big-head, stupid Dwight, and then I stopped. Kicked him in the head. Went for more but stopped.

I stopped and looked up the hill. On the steps, in front of the glassed-in porch, was Salty and older cousin Brian and younger cousin Brian, Skamper and Petie and Great-uncle Midas. They were all laughing. Holding themselves. "The runt beat his ass," Cousin Skamper said, smiling 'cause he knew he wasn't gonna be in the corner no more.

Dwight was in a ball crying and there was dried sweat and blood caking on my face and I was itching all over, all over everywhere, burning and itching and burning, burning, burning so I couldn't even start anywhere to get at it to make any of it stop. Great-uncle Midas and all the rest of them were up there falling over themselves laughing and laughing, and coming down from far up the sidewalk, way out a long blue car, were Preacher Porter with that ice bucket and Great-aunt Inola with that big ole switch, her now screaming, "Maceo! Boy, you come on over here right now," gliding down toward me fast with her silver cross swinging as I was itching everywhere, digging in with my dirty nails, trying to get at it everywhere.

I looked down and started walking the other way toward the big blue green mountains. Then up toward Midas and them. Then the mountains again, thinking on how I could get far, far away, knowing now I couldn't get far, far away as Great-uncle Midas laughed and laughed and Inola screamed and Preacher Porter boomed as I walked this way and walked that way and then just froze, feeling hot all over. Closing my eyes and covering my ears, hoping to disappear and not see or hear or feel any of it anymore, all the while itching and burning, looking everywhere, hoping maybe I might somehow catch the first thing smoking of my own and just ride and ride and ride and ride.

THE MAN ON THE
HOSPITAL BED

THE CAMERAMAN MOVED IN ON THE EIGHT DRUMMERS
banging four African beats as the three trumpets, two
trombones, and sax swung hard over the swinging rhythms
as the three old men took turns getting up out of their
chairs to pump life into the ballroom by singing on and on
and on. The sun rising with the bass thump in your chest as
people jammed up together, sweating, nearly naked, moving slowly, quickly, shaking, twisting, bending, on samba
toes, with sexy eyes, and licking lips, and smiles, all around
the big ballroom, up in the balconies, one woman with
Brazilian blue-painted breasts riding a thin rail so you
could see the better part of her ass, how it touched and
slid along. Another camera was there moving around her,
getting it all as a man and woman slipped in from behind,
smiling, feeling the blue breasts as another one now held
her legs wide open, with his tongue out near the rail, with
another on her neck as she swayed almost out of rhythm
with flamenco hands above her head, smiling big for the
camera, and "Exquisite," Hans said for the second time,
watching her, just as I figured he would, just as he'd done
all night. Outwitting chance and leading it by the hand
and a knock against my leg and there in the hospital bed

with wheels they shook the man in the yellow Speedo with baby arms and no legs and claw feet to the bass thump of the big bass drum beating through everyone dancing and drinking inside and out. You could smell the liquor coming out of the sweat of the men and women moving as many hands spun his wheeled bed as the crowd bounced on toes and shook shoulders and danced, singing and circling him and now not circling him, so you could see the left side of his face, soft like Silly Putty, molded as if mushed by many heavy fingers, his face discolored black to purple, all pushed in and smiling. I couldn't take my eyes off the left side of his face, burned badly, drooping down past his chin with drool rolling out of his mouth, his glasses sitting on a knob that was the leftovers of his ear. One of them, shaking her big ass in a tight white nurse's uniform, zipper down for cleavage, with long brown legs and a white hat and all, tried to pour *cachaça* into his drooling mouth, liquor all over his pillow, down the sides of his face. But he seemed to like it, singing louder, knowing all of the words, flopping on the cot, trying to sit up with those little arms to sing louder as a cameraman filmed and laughed and danced, trying to hold the nurse's hand. She froze. The cameraman slapped her ass. She frowned but everybody there cheered and laughed and circled her and then were not circling her as the man on the hospital bed glared like he would've done something if there were something he could do, but what could he do? He screamed. Those close stopped and stared and started moving again to the singing and swinging drums. He was sweating much now and the nurse leaned way down, brushing body with breast, to dab at his forehead.

With her bent over in that short dress, you could see. She moved around him and I looked at her face as she stroked his bald head, and his yellow Speedo moving as his baby fingers crawled underneath her dress. She stood up and froze but he was smiling big now and just kept doing it.

NINTH GRADE

BENEATH THE BLUE FLUORESCENT LIGHTS THE TOPS OF my hands looked olive, yellow, blue, like a bruise, having lost all of the copper brown from the indoors and weak winter sun. Ms. Wastpee, who was white, had me stuck all the way up front so she could watch me, she said, 'cause I couldn't be treated like an adult, she said, which was all bullshit, I'd said, which got me another month of special detention with the principal, Dr. Nelms, who was white, too. Old white Ms. Wastpee had me stuck all up front, so I could see all those small brown bumps beneath that thick spread of makeup and the red hairs sprouting from the mole on her neck and all the little breakfast things in between her urine-yellow teeth. She had me stuck all the way up front; and Preston, who was Tobagonian and black, all the way to the left; and Leonard, who was Jamaican and black, all the way to the right; and smiling white kids all in the middle; and Lebron, who was somewhere in between black and white, Lebron, who'd come in with the new kids, the only new one up in our classes, had him all the way in the back, which was good and fine 'cause he was small and frail and crazy and glared and kept saying he was gonna kick all our candy white-boy asses, which, if you ever saw him, with his thin wrists and little tiny feet, you'd know was more talk than anything.

With my friend white Kevin Greeley, giving the fuck-you finger to her back on the sly, his elbow nudging my side on the sneak, his tongue out far, licking his lips at her big fat ass, making me laugh, making me smile, old white Ms. Wastpee would always turn and see my giggles and his straight face and red pen moving fast, taking the notes from the blackboard. She'd smile and shake her head and lean down easy and whisper soft, "Maceo, you know who to see, Maceo," with that egg salad breath of hers all about me, Kevin Greeley, smiling straight-faced, big eyes down like he hadn't done a thing.

That was the first year after the big court case. The year Leonard and me were still friends and Preston was still alive. The year they had to watch and see what redrawing and widening and busing in those from way down the hill, down, down, where all the hills went flat and the houses were run-down and small with boarded-up windows, down near bombed-out Irvington, East Orange, Newark, down where nearly everyone moving was dark and everyone walking walked along level roads without any fear of ever seeing anyone white. That was the year those types of whites that had moved to get as far away as they could but really hadn't gotten that far away and couldn't afford to get any farther away, couldn't afford one of those private schools, weren't good enough for one of those private-school sports scholarships, had to sit and wait and watch and see what would happen with those dark folks they had just gotten away from coming high up into the hills for the better education, mixing up everybody like everyone was all the same.

We lived at the top of one of the hills, above everyone and everything, with a lot of yard and a view of everything all the way to the Twin Towers in New York City. My mother, who was light-skinned and a lawyer, wasn't sure what to make of any of it, those new ones who'd just come to school from the flatlands all around me, affecting me, how they talked and dressed and reflected on us, us having just moved respectably from New York City, my mother sometimes having notions along the lines of old white Ms. Wastpee's notions. Some days my mother thought it might do me some good to have other American blacks around me at my school. Good for me to see the difference between me and them. Good motivation to work a lot harder. Good to see and appreciate all the good things they'd given me. Good to have some black girls around for me to look at, too.

But some days, weekend days mostly, Sundays after church really, after she'd had two solid days of family time to really think hard on it, that all went out of her. She'd ome home and lay her purse down slow on the big chair in the living room and you could see it all running about her mind. Sunday nights at the dinner table over London broil and green beans with no TV running, she'd wonder aloud about the bits of stories from the gossip and long talks from after Saint George's Episcopal that had made their way to her ears. Maybe no, she'd begin to think as she wondered on the black and white fights and waylays and this person and that person whose mother she knew who'd been beaten down and bloodied and left on lawns here and there, she'd begin to say, "I'm not sure," and, "Maybe," and, "Perhaps." She'd look up from her half-finished plate and over to me. I'd smile at her.

She'd smile over my head at the trees and look down. Her face would loosen. "But," she'd say, "but you keep your grades up," she'd say, "so we don't have to send you to Exeter," she'd say, sort of smiling as my father, who'd jumped out of planes at night as a ranger in the army in Vietnam and hadn't ever wanted to move to New Jersey and was most certainly black, shook his head and looked out our big living-room bay window, down the hills, over the bare and swaying icicled trees, out toward the skyline of New York, where he and my mother still worked.

"Not a goddamn safe place in the world. And what the hell do trees and grass do ya, anyway?" you could sometimes hear him say at the windows if you were close.

All Leonard, Preston, and me knew was now we wouldn't be the only black kids in school.

Early in the mornings we'd come inside from the cold gray days in big coats and scarves, salt mixed with melting snow on the tops of our shoes. We'd come in from long, wet walks cold and early, rubbing bare hands and stomping numb feet, to stand around and watch one another while pretending not to be looking at one another, waiting and watching the black kids wiping off the shells and soles of their shell-toed Adidases with the fat Skittles-colored laces, which always matched the color of their Skittles-colored Lee jeans. We'd mostly stand around watching one another, waiting for the black kids and the clear sound of Our Lady of Sorrows' ten cathedral bells drifting from across the other end of the frozen duck pond where a lotta the white Irish and Italian kids went to church and the bigger black and white fights would go on after school. We'd wait for those ten bells to ring softly, telling us before the school whistle, telling us all, the long day of school was about to begin. All the black and white kids would come inside the glass doors and rub and stomp and stand and wait for the bells together but separate, bunched in small groups in the front hall in front of the ten big wooden auditorium doors, right where the Ping-Pong Club set up the ten Ping-Pong tables right after school.

Early in the mornings, in the big front lobby, stomping, waiting, watching, you could hear the white boys whispering things and see the pretty black girls and all the pretty white girls in all the grades and maybe get close to the bunches of them standing around far and near in small circles watching the black kids' rapping and popping and breaking and glaring and threatening one or two of the smirking white kids they'd heard were whispering things about them being niggers and there being too many of them in our school. The black kids in wool hats and gloves would spin on their heads and hands on the wet floor. Up and dancing and swaying, laughing, yelling, smiling in circles, watching one another's bright colors, down on backs spinning and spinning. Black hair singed straight. Smells of steam heat and Jheri Curl swirls. Yellow laces and raspberry lollipops and laughing smiles laced with gold. Up and swaying with white towels around their necks, wiping their heads, doing the wave with big gold nameplates swinging and pretty white and black girls aahing and oohing. White towels wiping the soles and tops of wet shoes, and perfectly white shells floating and gliding, sliding the moon walk across wet brown boot tracks. With all eyes big and watching, three of them there always doing a colorful helicopter right at the drifting bells before we all went inside for our day.

Lebron would stand over near a glass door and pop and pop and pop and he was good but everybody black and white would turn and laugh at him there, tiny, trying to dance black.

When it came up, most kids agreed there was a good chance Lebron's father might be some kind of black 'cause of Lebron's broad nose and Lebron's walnut color from all the summer sun right at the beginning of school. Most kids around school agreed Lebron's father might be some kind of black but he'd gone off somewhere. Nobody from either school had ever seen him. Not that that meant anything. But his mother looked white if you ever caught a good look at her, dressed white for sure, which was more than enough for most anybody who cared and was looking. And with his green eyes, tufts of straight hair, winter skin the color of wheat, Lebron would deny it all, rapping and popping alone over to the sides of all the circles of fresh black kids he'd come in with, with his white-and-black shell-toed Adidas and fat cherry-red laces matching his cherry-red Lee jeans, with the black kids there early in the mornings, turning from time to time to laugh hard and tell him loud he couldn't do nothing right, his mama was most certainly white, which most certainly made him a whitey, too.

Oreo, they'd call him.

Zebra, they'd say.

White boy, they'd grin.

And he'd droop his head so you could see the many bald spots where the welts and scars from the fire wouldn't let the hair grow anymore. He'd droop his head, and "No," he'd say. "Cuban," he'd say. "High Haitian," he'd say. "Egyptian," he'd say. "Moorish, Persian, Spanish from the south of Spain," he'd sometimes say when they wouldn't stop.

The white kids, with their long-sleeved pastel Polos and fancy digital watches, liked to weave their way all among the circles and circles of people and get close to him, right behind him, right as the church bells would begin to ring. They liked to get right close to him as he stopped popping and began watching over the backs of all the wool-hatted heads, the colorful whirl-whirl of the helicopter going around and around and around, and say not too loud and not too soft, with hands over their mouths as if to cough, "Patch Head! Patch Head! Spic!" smiling with one another as if they hadn't said a thing at all and nobody but themselves could tell they'd done it.

Leonard, Preston, and me would stand somewhere in between all of this, sort of peering but not looking too much 'cause none of us really wanted the early-morning attention. All the morning monitors, who were always white 'cause they were teachers, always stood by the black kids, letting them spin and twist and carry on across the wet floors. The morning monitors would stand very close to one another and grimace from time to time 'cause it was early and cold and they could hear all the things they were trying hard not to hear. They'd heard early on how Jimmy Lowell, who was black and bigger than all of them, had picked up the desk above his head and hurled it across the room at Mrs. Obeia, who was white and small and French and taught French and liked to say some of the bad things she really thought about them, 'cause I guess that's what they can do over there in Paris, France. They got rid of him but there was a lot of Jimmy

Lowells left there dancing and swaying and gold-tooth smiling there in the front hall in the mornings. They'd hear of the music teacher Mr. Lion putting all the cute new black girls on his lap to teach them jazz piano chords. Ms. Crest giving A's to the tall ones with big hands in the corner of the room.

The white kids went left and the black kids right, and sometimes the white kids would watch the black kids break-dance and spin from afar and sometimes the white girls would giggle and smile at the black boys, which nobody, including the monitors, were quite sure what to do with.

Candice D'Amico, who was white but giggled watching the black boys, broke up with Kevin Greeley, who was good looking and Irish and white with blue eyes, Irish black hair and a big limp he'd had since birth. Irish Kevin didn't like any of it, Candice telling him it was over. They'd gone out for three years and he said they had love and Candice was real pretty with nice big tits and long legs and an apple for an ass, which made everyone, teachers and students, whites and blacks, girls and boys, always look, want, and wonder. Candice, who was Italian and sorta olive colored, started going out with a rich, new, sharp, paper-bag-brown-colored Brazilian kid named Otavio who didn't understand and thought it was all silly but played soccer with us and had a nice big smile, which made a lotta the girls, both black and white, look, want, and redden. All the white boys started calling her slut and word spread around that the only reason Otavio went out with her was 'cause she gave it up, and then the white girls said that Otavio had a big Brazilian dick and Latin-lover moves and that's what it was for Candice.

Otavio and Candice would walk around the halls and hold hands. The black kids would stop and look long at them both and try to catch his eyes so he'd know, but he didn't know or didn't care, maybe. He'd just walk and look at Candice and smile. After a while the black kids whistled and called him worse names than anything me, Preston, and Leonard ever got. The white kids just tried to ignore Candice, like it didn't mean a thing, but she was real good looking and so that got to getting them, too. Nobody anywhere was sure what to do. So we all just watched.

At lunch all the black kids would go left and all the white kids right, sitting together but separate, in clusters, in little black and white groups, to the left and right at the many fold-down, one-piece, park-bench-style gray plastic tables. A black side. A white side. All the frowning lunch monitors, who were teachers, would mill around on the black side, grimacing 'cause it was loud and they heard things they wished they hadn't heard. Heard the loud talk and laughing and different English and cursing and threats of fights and bad, hard words for the teachers who didn't treat people right, and every day of Ralph Cobb, who was black and sold drugs and every day wore a mink coat to school, loud and long and hard so anyone could hear about sweet Ralph Cobb, who they'd finally gotten with a school-placed pistol set beneath a ton of books in his locker, and we all knew the things that had happened 'cause Ralph was smart and had been at it a long time and never carried a gun or any drugs ever anywhere on his person, and so the monitors would look around, look at one another, clench their jaws, and shift from foot to foot 'cause they didn't want any gun trouble or fights or security guards or metal detectors like there were in Irvington, East Orange, Newark. And they could hear it all loudly and it was much later in the day and they were tired, and that's when everyone began to have enough and the bad things would really start to happen. The lunch monitors, who were mostly the big teachers, so white men, would just stand around and look and mumble and grumble and shake their heads and cross their arms, glaring, scowling, eyeing, watching the black left side.

Leonard and me would go on the end of our friends' table, the white boys' table sometimes, like we had in grammar school, sometimes, as the fights got worse, by ourselves behind the white girls' table, with gentle whispers of "those niggers" slipping down to slow and sting no matter where we were sitting, with little white-boy nods and metal-brace grins, meaning those words weren't meant for us but the other ones, the new ones, the poor ones from the flatlands, on the other side of the cafeteria, talking loud and different. Kevin Greeley would always look at us there and come down and sit with us there, trying to explain to us how nobody meant anything in what they were saying and how they didn't really understand and like a snowball downhill once people started talking that way and what could be expected when all our friends were getting hurt and beaten up bad. He'd smile and pat our backs and sometimes that would make it sorta all right, him there with us, saying he understood, or at least there trying hard to understand.

The white girls, the pretty ones, too, would all come around when he came around our end of the table and they'd sit and try to get his attention by trying to talk to Preston and me and Leonard. But he would never hear them. Never see them, looking only over to where brown-bag Otavio and his olive Candice were leaning in close to each other, sitting and eating and touching hands and kissing ears. You could hear her, when they sat close by us, giggling, trying to wag her finger Brazilian style the way he did, say things in Portuguese the way Otavio tried to teach us all, both black and white, when we stretched at soccer practice.

Candice and Otavio would sit alone with each other at lunch at a table by the window in the far corner over on the left sometimes, or near the front door near us sometimes, on the right sometimes, and I think that got everybody old, young the most, them sitting there touching, really not hearing any of those nasty words and eyes getting hurled their way. Lebron would sit at the end of their table no matter where they sat. Otavio was nice to Lebron sometimes in the mornings in class. Otavio, who could sit anywhere he liked, would sit back there with Lebron in old white Ms. Wastpee's class. Lebron and Octavio were about the same color, really, if you looked, really, in the wintertime under those blue fluorescent lights. Around the halls Otavio said some words to him sometimes, told him jokes, and you could see Lebron laugh big so you could see his bursting buck teeth he tried to hide all the time with his hands. Candice started to, too, sit with them in the back of the class and make him laugh like that. A slow, high, bubbling giggle like you'd never heard. And Lebron would let them go on talking like he wasn't there and couldn't hear anything at lunch or walking around the halls or in classes, only smiling sometimes at the nice things they said to one another.

Candice's father, who was white and Italian and a big-wig government politician in Maplewood, all the time wearing thick glasses with a beard, going around making speeches, all the time in the paper smiling for things he'd just done, found out about the sitting and smiling and touching and things and beat Candice all around the mouth and eyes, so everything was big and swollen on her. She wore dark glasses over the black and blue. Caked makeup over the swells like how Ms. Wastpee would wear it. After some time she tried to sneak sitting and talking to Otavio and doing things with him but she got beaten up again all about the face and eyes, so she had those big, dark glasses on again that none of the teachers made her take off.

Her jaw and eyes got better and she stopped talking to Otavio but didn't take off the glasses and started carving *Def Leppard* and *Ozzy Osbourne* and *Brazil* big and deep all around her forearms with a Swiss Army pocketknife. She did it in Ms. Wastpee's English class and in Mr. Richter's biology class and Mrs. Lechters's government and politics class and, they say, a little at home, too, when no one was there, and she tried to wear long-sleeved shirts sometimes but you can't hide things like that long, and one day right in the middle of Mrs. Mirella's Latin class Dr. Nelms and some white lady in a suit with pants came and got her and she was gone, whisked right away in the middle of the school year. Everybody knew why but nobody said much except it happened and she wouldn't ever be coming back.

Early in the gray mornings cold, rubbing, stomping, pale white Irish, crippled Kevin Greeley, who knew judo or karate or something, would look over at us and back at his white friends and make tight smiles and lean in and whisper that it was poison black dick that made his Candice do those things and how she never would've done a thing like that if she had stayed true to her own, and he would look over at us and then the laughing and spinning and screaming and hollering and over at Lebron and Otavio by the glass doors and back to his circle of white friends and he'd shake his head and smile big, then make tight frowns like the morning monitors', and "Jigaboos," he'd gently say, "fucking monkeys," he'd whisper, shaking his head, big eyes watching.

FIVE-STAR HOTEL

THAT THIRD DAY THE THREE WOMEN IN WHITE FINALLY
said, "Bom dia," with real smiles when he stepped in front
of me like a policeman trying to shoo me away from the
hotel door. Hard Brazilian looks, fingers on my arm, words
he shouldn't have been saying to anyone. The doorman
wasn't so big but held me firm as expensive people went
in and out of the glass sliding doors. The doors hummed
sharp, half opening and closing from the uneven pressure
of his left foot. He was pushing but I was pushing back.
His withered face. An old man before his time. The unfor-
giving sun. I finally let him move me when he pushed
hard to move me, 'cause he seemed like he might call some
others over for help and I've always liked to see what
these kinds of people will do alone when they think they
can do anything. My nodding to his mumblings as we went
not fast but slow toward the women in blood-splattered
dresses with blood-spotted turbans, dirty and sitting on the
curb over a big side of meat in a big plastic bag that leaked
blood in lines off the curb into pools by their bunioned bare
feet. Skewer piles by their side, strays watching and waiting, the cold grill, the hot heat, their hands massaging
the brown meat, and despite his mumblings, him, what he
did, I still can't get their squishing fingers outta my mind.

The meat smelled everywhere. The youngest woman, almost a girl, hardly moved, off to the side, in some shade, clean in her all-whites, and when she turned to look at me, a baby feeding at her breast, her long white dress let down to her stomach, her shoulder naked to the sun. That shoulder smooth, the color of the night. Beautiful. She smiled at me. The baby's head stirring calmly, the woman watching me closely while I watched her. They all watched me. Us. Him moving me slowly, all the while their kneading hands squishing, when the young one stood quick and smiling and then not smiling but screaming something so fast and hard I didn't understand. He let go of my arm and started at them but now I held him by the arm. His soft smile burrowing into his twisting face as I leaned in close, speaking loud English fast so the sweat grew in the gray hairs between his ear and blue doorman's hat. Her baby was crying now. Kicking.

AT THE SAME TIME ON THE SIXTH DAY, COMING OUT OF the hotel, there he was smiling big at me, putting his arm around my waist, walking me along like we were now old friends. There I was again letting him walk me when he walked me, 'cause I've always liked to see what these kinds of people will do when they know they shouldn't have done what they did and might pay for it. "And my three friends?" I said, pointing. "Oof," he only said, and "Oof," again in a high voice. And then leaning in close with English, "In the United States they not like the black man"—shaking his head—"but Brazil, oof. Black man drive a nice car, dress nice, play football, sing music, people say, 'Yes, Doctor,' 'Look good, Doctor,' 'What you want, Doctor,' 'What I get you, Doctor.' The black woman scared to try for a man like you or I. They know all the rich will have the white. No one remember. No one care. I often forget my skin," smiling with his fat hand on my back, walking me slowly along past the lines of dried blood baked onto the sidewalk where he'd once allowed them to be.

UNCLE RAYMOND

HE'S GOT HIS NEW WINTER COAT ON WITH THOSE HEAD-phones blasting real loud, blasting so loud we can all hear clear the words to all the songs, as he just sits there with his big brown body shlumped up at the kitchen table, with his hazel eyes going googily at everything while grinning, sweating, laughing, yawning real wide with all his yellow teeth flashing as he giggles and drinks his beer and click-click-flicks through the TV channels and crosses and uncrosses his legs, to sit back in his stool and jerk forward and lean slowly back and smile and fiddle with his Walkman and laugh and frown and jerk, jerk, jiggle, sway, looking left, right, down, up, behind, out at the falling snow through the window, to smile for a while at nothing I can make out from here. He's just sitting there flicking, drinking, sweating, smiling, frowning, grinning, jerking, easing, fiddling, crossing, uncrossing, looking here and there slowly and quickly at everything and nothing, red drunk eyes, dazed like he's never seen it before and won't ever see it again, as his left hand rests calm across his big, bulging belly with a drooping half-ashed cigarette in between his uncut fingernails like a weed roach. Most everybody else sitting up there with him at my grandma's long kitchen-counter table try to pay him no mind, but I see him.

I watch him. They keep on talking loud around him, trying to smile and laugh through him and the time by way of good gossip, old stories, and sweet lies. Then somebody'll nudge him, "Raymond," and he looks around and smiles and ashes his cigarette.

"Take that coat off," Grandma says.

Uncle Raymond is up there fidgeting in his brand-new white high-top Christmas sneakers laced too tight and new blue Christmas coat with a furry hood like Eskimos wear, up there thinking folks are going to let him slide out again to get some more beer, but company is coming. Family. Friends. And the liquor makes it worse.

"Those headphones off and that coat right back in the box where you found it," she says, but Raymond just looks out the window while burning through the channels.

From my grandpa's big rose chair in the living room, alone, near the blinking tree, I just sit and watch. Eighteen and full with promise. They think whatever it is they did, whatever it is older people do to younger people to make them a certain right way, had somehow come together in me. Had stuck and taken and now there were big hopes. Things to learn from. Uncles and aunts would touch me and smile when I came around, a hand on the shoulder, an arm around the waist with lots of last-minute dos and don'ts to tweak the many hours of work they'd put in me over the many long Flint summers to get me where I was going, an Ivy League school my mother had let them believe was paying me to play soccer for them, which, of course, wasn't all true.

*   *   *

EVERYBODY'S GOT AN OPINION BUT NOBODY KNOWS FOR sure what went wrong with Raymond, which is to say the exact when and how he started straddling worlds and then one day just slipped this one altogether for some place else entirely. But what almost everybody who needs to know knows for certain is what my uncle Otis, by way of Arkansas, and my aunt Corine like to lean in and say come holiday times with a soft Little Rock drawl and candy-coated Crown Royal breath, "Rayyyyyymond's breaaaaaad ain't done," which is to say Raymond is a little off, which is, of course, very true.

Holiday times when some friends and distant family folks who aren't familiar with things come to visit and Grandma and Grandpa get up out of earshot and Raymond gets going grinning and jerking with his eyes going everywhere most Joyner quick to say with a wink and a smile, "Raymond ain't truly one of us," which is to mean he's adopted, which is probably mostly true, too. It seems to put other folks at ease some. Somewhere down deep it seems to put all the rest of us family folk at ease, too, for depending on who and what you believe, we all seem to think some horrible thing like that could never happen to the likes of us for coming from a different, better, sturdier stock of people.

Ever since my grandma fell that last time and broke her hip, she doesn't move too good but uses a cane and never sits up at the kitchen counter with everybody anymore but down in her low chair with wheels by the wall. From there she can still smile sometimes, seeing almost everyone she helped raised, which means all of us. She has stories, good squirming hot-seat stories, on everybody that she lays out from time to time when someone gets on someone else a little too hard. She gets going telling and everyone goes quiet listening as her almond-shaped Egyptian eyes like mine get small, then big, as she travels back through the years, forgetting where she is, down in that low chair. Her face softens over the stories of all of us as she gets going back, and further back when Raymond was young and going to do something great, making her wish for those times when Raymond could listen and smile right along with us, telling his own brand of great big ole gut-splitting lies he learned directly from years of listening and laughing while riding over to the north side with my granddaddy in that beat-up faded blue Ford pickup truck to fix Ms. Fat Butt's busted toilet or some other house Granddaddy owned over on Spencer Street on the north side of Flint. Before Raymond lost it, he used to be not just Grandma's favorite, but Granddaddy's favorite, too. His protégé.

From the low chair Grandma can get up and out to do things around the kitchen easier and to make it nice. My cousin Sidney put an old rotary phone like how she likes right there next to her down low on the wall with a long, long cord and one of those shoulder rests for when her friends call and get talking and she doesn't want to get up but wheels slowly here and there about the kitchen, pushing the volume down on the TV when Raymond has it high and isn't listening or can't hear her asking or something. When we all get together, that's where she sits, right there by the old phone, but it's not the same. Grandma still doesn't want to believe it happened to her like this—not her hip, but Raymond, her baby, the way he is. And when it comes on her, you can see it coming from everywhere.

*　　*　　*

THE SMOKED TURKEY, REGULAR TURKEY, HONEYED HAM,
are cooking in the oven and big pots of greens and baked
beans, green beans, gravy, pans of corn bread, corn bread
stuffing, mac and cheese, sweet potatoes, rolls, are warming on top of the stove with steam oozing out of other
pots, all smelling of good things to come with the pound
cake, apple pie, sweet potato pie, pumpkin pie, derby pie,
sock-it-to-me cake, coconut cake, cheesecake, and German chocolate cake cooling on a counter in the dining
room. My aunts have been cooking for three days in four
separate houses. It's snowing pretty hard outside, white
on green, big flakes weighing down branches, evergreen
leaves sagging toward the ground. Raymond is sitting still
in his coat but zooming through the channels at the speed
of light, grinning and laughing at something only he sees
out in those trees. The younger cousins and women are
moving quickly around the house and kitchen. Dishes,
forks, knives, are clinking and clanking out of the dish-
water, against one another, as cabinets swing open and
bang closed with the vacuum going on loud above everything but the TV. Like every year, the women are doing
the things to get ready for the other friends, family, folks,
coming soon. It's going to be a big meal.

The men and my mother are sitting and talking and
laughing up at the kitchen counter. Every now and then
an aunt or someone will take a break and sit for a while
with them and my ma and let a story loose on somebody
or something and laugh hard along with everyone else.
This is how it's been every year for as long as I can re-

member. Nobody wondering, but falling and settling right into the same ways and grooves waiting right there for them from the last year's Christmas. Grandma is frowning at Raymond, wanting him to take off his coat and act different and right and not so sick but the way how he was supposed to be. Nobody else sees but it seems she wants someone else to get on Raymond with that sweating from that coat.

Folks are feeling something, telling longer, louder lies and better stories above the TV and laughing hard and often, so Raymond's grinning and laughing almost seems in time and all right but it's not. Grandma isn't having it. I can hear his headphones from here, and when he laughs, it's deep and hard and would stop anyone who didn't know the shape of things. All of it is getting Grandma real good, so her eye is jumping and her mouth is bursting loaded nothings as she looks around at everyone moving here and there quickly, the way Raymond sometimes gets to looking around at everything and nothing. Her phone is ringing loud the way Sidney fixed it, and she leans to get it and then stops and from the low chair starts in on him, soft to loud, "Raymond, Raymond, Raymonnnnnd," as the old, big black phone rings and rings but he doesn't hear any of that stuff out of her anymore but grins and stands up and sits back down and grabs one of his four cigarettes lying on the counter and then his lighter. Now leaning back with smoke coming out of his nostrils, rubbing the top of his hair so dandruff and brown things are falling over his shoulders. She's yelling, the phone ringing, everyone talking, his headphones blaring, the vacuum on loud, then off as she yells, then on loud, and "Raymond, Raymond, Raymond," and off, but it's not for him she's screaming. He looks and looks away out at the snow on the trees as the phone rings and the TV belches pieces of loud sound. He grins and kicks his wet white new no-name Christmas sneakers against the metal foot bar like he's gone outside already as her phone rings, back and forth, so there's a rhythmic basketball squeak back and forth with some tune he's hearing from far away, and "Boy, what's so funny, turn that off, Raymond, turn them headphones off, Raymond! Raymond!" she says, and he stands up, and "What are you listening to, Raymond?" I say loud above everything.

" 'Bitches Brew,' " he says, " 'Bitches Brew,' " without looking back at me, "Miles sucking all the juice out of them notes," he says, "Herbie Hancock settin' him up nice with them chords," he says, "Electricity," he says as all of his uncles and brothers sitting there go quiet, stop. Look. The phone is ringing and the vacuum from somewhere in the back of the house low, then louder, then low again as someone goes on too loud about weather in the Ohio valley on TV. Raymond sits and takes a drag and lets the smoke come out of his nose. "Daddy, I need a beer," he says. "It's not time," I hear my granddaddy's voice, and Raymond stands and "Can anyone run me 'round to the gas station?" he says, and sits and yawns through his teeth. "Ain't time and not open," Cousin Benella says. The phone stops ringing. Grandma just watches him. Raymond jerks forward and grins and laughs. "I'm gonna go out soon," he says, and gets up off the stool and rubs his hands and sits back down and grins at the snow while smoke comes out his mouth in rings, and my grandma says, "Not for any beer. Raymond, why don't you help set the plates and take that coat off and help somebody, someone needs help, why don't you help Elton, Elton needs help with—"

"It's not time yet, Raymond," Granddaddy booms louder over Grandma.

"Ain't nobody gonna take you anywhere on Christmas, so you might as well take that coat off, Raymond," my cousin Betty says.

"Can't nobody run you over there, Raymond, with all these people coming, know you're not suppose to drink, so don't know why you're asking," my mother says loud, almost for show, touching Raymond's shoulder, then pulling on the shoulder of the coat. Raymond grins at something. Shakes his shoulder to help my mother. One sleeve comes off and he sits back into his stool, blows smoke out the side of his mouth. My mother shakes her head. Dips back into the every-year-overheated conversation about who was and is the more benevolent and credible, Muhammad or Jesus, my uncle Langston pushing the conversation, being the youngest of my mother's siblings besides Raymond, and now the understood smartest, but still living in my grandma's basement as some sort of a kind of devout Nation of Islam Muslim in a house of every-Sunday-going-to-church Baptists. It gets my grandma every year. Raymond knows we'll all be back into our other lives in a few days. Uncle Langston's son, Cousin Elton, who is not a Muslim but is four years younger than me and the actual one who quietly does most of the last-minute Christmas cooking, says Raymond just waits and acts good for the four days when my mother is in town watching him, then goes right back to how he was before she came. Raymond is no fool. My second cousin Audrey, who always comes early, even with her young baby, to help Elton with the cutting and salad prepping and anything else anyone wants her to do, says she's sure Raymond is going to get better, 'cause there's so much love in Aunt Estelle Joyner's house, this house, and they all go to church—or mosque, in Uncle Langston's case—and pray, so things will work themselves out by way of God's love, but she has to say stupid things like that 'cause she married somebody white and wants folks to say a few words to him, give him a chance. Raymond picks up the remote and leans back and crosses his legs and starts in on the channels fast as ever with one sleeve of his jacket brushing the floor, so you can see the orange inside as he sometimes jerks.

My grandma watches him and starts up again, "Raymond! Raymond! Raymonnnd!" Like nothing's just happened. He's sweating. He freezes. Eyes wide like he's heard something. Stands up. Starts quick down the hall toward his room with his jacket half-on, one sleeve dragging and my grandma screaming after him and it's too much for the folks up there and cousins, uncles, brothers, nephews are trying hard not to hear it the way Raymond doesn't hear it, trying to forget by talking louder and laughing harder so as not to have to see what Grandma sees, hoping it all might just up and fly away and "Raymond, Raymonnnnd," she's half standing up, leaning on the arm of her chair for support which means she means it, "And take that coat off, boy, and put it back in the box where you found it back under that tree," she yells but Raymond is long gone and everybody sitting is now getting up and looking down quiet. Back at her and around again for another place to get up and go to help somebody do something around the house out of the kitchen, 'cause we all know what comes next when Grandma starts getting this way, feeling mad and sad about taking Raymond in, having him still around at her age, wondering while knowing why nobody will take him who can and should take him, everyone quietly knowing full well how hard it is for her to get around to make sure of him these days, knowing she won't be able to do it much longer.

"Maceo," she says not so loud, "go and make Raymond a plate," as she sits and reaches for the black phone, "and tell him to put that coat and shoes back away in his Christmas box and come back out here, 'cause folks are coming soon want to see him," 'cause she knows I'll do it and not ask her any reason why and Raymond sometimes says a word to me from time to time and maybe she was hoping.

See, must be nearly forty folks between the Joyners, Hiltons, and Browns, all living close by one another in Flint. Least four families could stand to have Raymond. She knows it's not the money and she's right. She's got plenty saved special for when the time comes she's not around, money for this time now when she can't do it. She knows we all know this, too. But she starts getting that way screaming, "Raymond, Raymond, Raymonnnd," hovering around saying something else nobody wants to hear, shake things outside the groove and spoil the day and time and people stop talking and smiling and start noticing Raymond and remembering and watching her face while slowly getting up and slinking to do all that needs to be done 'cause it's holiday time. Christmas Day.

The truth is nobody wants to go through it all over again, hear Grandma start asking her whys and why nots and find themselves the one having to say the reasons to her out loud again. Not at Christmas. But really, I guess, not ever.

Because Raymond lies and steals from Grandma's purse and Granddaddy's wallet and picks the locked closet where the valuables get put away to and nods off and falls asleep in chairs and beds with cigarettes still burning in between his fingers and sometimes forgets to put his sticky nudie books away under the sink and leaves them right by the toilet, where even my grandma can see them, and says "Yes, all right" and "All right, yes" or nothing at all with his Walkman roaring to anyone who says "Don't do this" and "You gotta do that," and the one time my granddaddy went a little crazy himself and had a shovel and was really going to do something bad banging on Raymond's locked door, Uncle Langston ran upstairs and talked Granddaddy out of the shovel and then Grandma stopped talking to Granddaddy for a week saying "That's not what you do with someone who needs help." Cousin Benella, who's just about Raymond's age and actually might know, says quiet but often, "Raymond don't want to get no better. Happy just where he is. Ain't gonna let that fool burn me up. Stealing from me in my own house, PLEASE! Shoulda done somethin' while they had the chance to do somethin'."

They say it wasn't always like that, Raymond crazy. I can still remember when he'd come out of it, *whap*. You never knew how long it'd last. That was long ago when I was barely eight and Raymond's face wasn't so soft and round and his gut didn't jut out over his belt buckle and he didn't drink quite how he drinks all the time nowadays.

He'd be watching the TV or in his room or even during Christmas dinner gnawing on a turkey bone or something, burning nonstop through the stations with those headphones screaming Miles, fidgeting and grinning, looking at his thumb moving the remote button, and then up to the space where his cigarette smoke disappeared to and *whap*, he'd just stop and look around clear. You could see it. His eyes. He'd look around all clear for a moment. Get up and go without a word to stand right in front of his Hammond B3 organ still waiting for him in the living room. Pull his headphones down around his neck and move the sound down real low so not even he could hear. Sit down for a minute not doing anything. Turn the organ on. Close his eyes, listening to it purr as it warmed. Back straight, head cocked to the side as if hearing something coming from the sky. Eyes open and a smile and just like that he'd start playing and playing and playing and playing with his eyes closed and head all the way back as his body rocked slow and swayed hard like Ray Charles, shoulders dancing, long basketball fingers jumping, floating, plunging, swinging up and down the white and black keys as his feet bounced and roared jazzy, bluesy, gospel bass lines down along the many wooden bass foot pedals, to turn around and look at us while slowly, slowly sliding back into a church hymn he knew made my grandma smile and quickly feet bouncing back into something bopping again for the rest of us and "Watch him," my dad would say, "his feet, his feet playing the bass, watch him, watch him," he'd say as everybody in and out of my grandma's house would stop whatever it was they were doing and follow the music to stand all around the back of him to watch and sway and listen, enjoying the small time he was back here with us, the older folks thinking of when Raymond was young and gifted with prospects, back when he was with promise and potential and sane and always in this world, us young, young kids wanting to reach out and touch him to see if he was real, while wondering how in the world anybody, 'specially crazy Raymond, could play anything that sounded so good out of the big brown monster of an organ nobody else ever went near. But that was long ago. Eleven years.

I knock on his door. Thin sounds of music coming from his headphones through the door, smoke from under it, smells of cigarette ash mixed with turkey, honeyed ham, and gravy, and laughing and talking wafting warm from the living room and kitchen down the hall.

"Raymond," I say but there's nothing, and "Raymond," I say, "you all right, man? I got a plate a food here for you from Grandma," but only smoke from under his door, the tin sound of some headphone's horn coming through softly. I try the doorknob, and "Everything taste terrible," I hear him say, and the knob won't turn. Locked.

"What happened?" I say, and "Terrible," I hear, "Horrible right on the tongue," he says real loud, "Okay," he says, "okay," he says, "wait," he says, "wait," and then nothing but the horn from his headphones, smells of smoke and ash from under his door.

"Grandma wants you to take that coat off and those shoes and put 'em back in your Christmas box," I say. "I'll help if you want. Whatta ya say, ya all right?" I say, my ear pressed to his locked door, listening. "Ya okay?" Listening for something, anything else. "What ya listening to?" I ask. But nothing.

I wait.

Nothing.

What will I tell her?

After a while, "Ya want me to leave this plate out here?"

I say, but he's gone, gone to that other place. Or maybe just out his window like I guess he sometimes must do. I take his plate to the bathroom window, bring it back clean to his door in case someone else comes to look and see.

MY MOTHER SAYS SHE AND MY AUNT CORINE WERE PRAC-tically grown when my grandparents took Raymond in. Nobody knows why they did it. Folks say things because folks always say things, but now it's hard to know what to believe. Grandma isn't always so nice. Says "no" real hard in many ways, and the rest of us tend to tell lies and some-times all that can come leaking out of folks in the many ways they tell about Raymond.

But Granddaddy and Grandma had four kids already and were poor and working hard in the GM plants, hav-ing to stretch things to keep it together, when talk of a new child started bubbling around the house. There was a neighbor and she was from Pine Bluff, Arkansas, like my grandfolks were, and had come north, to Michigan, to Flint, with her husband for the work at the plants and it had all gone to shit on her. Her husband was dead or gone or something, wasn't around, is how my uncle Louis the dentist says it. The woman, the neighbor, was coal black and had no job and no prospects and decided she had bet-ter go on back to whatever it was she had left behind. She gave Raymond to my grandfolks. My grandfolks took him in. "It was a different time back then" is how my uncle Langston the Muslim mumbles it. My mother will say she and Corine raised Raymond and Grandma had no busi-ness taking on more than she could but that's what she says and sometimes my mother can say and not say a lot depending on what she wants you to think or know.

My mother, who's the first and at least fifteen years older, says for a while everyone in the immediate and extended family thought Raymond was going to outshine all the kids and even her brothers and sisters and cousin Benella knew it. He was talking before anybody else had and walking before anybody and had that music; she says he was always good with the music, used to play Sundays for the church and had made the varsity basketball team as a sophomore at Northern and was long, lean, and handsome with those almond-shaped hazel eyes like mine and Grandma's. Raymond had lots of friends and girlfriends and was a smart boy going to college. Everyone boasted, talked of him, touched him, sure he'd do the family right.

And then he came apart.

Cousin Benella says Uncle Raymond was losing it even at the end of high school, at Northern. She says he ran with a certain crowd she wouldn't go near, which are the things nobody else knows or at least says. Benella says they were watching TV and he told her he was hearing the voices sometimes, sometimes those voices, those people in his head, would come around telling him what to do, not always good things either. "Oh, now ya don't even want to be in the room with me," he said, and then "I bet ya all scared, right?" and she says she said, "No," but as he said all this she was scared of him and his voices, and who can blame her? She says she remembers that and him telling her one day in high school, "Yeah, I don't ever plan to leave Mama and Daddy. I'm gonna get a factory job and just live on 'em at home." Benella says right on the heels of that, "I'm not sayin' Raymond ain't really sick but you know, I'm not sayin' he's tryin' his hardest to get better. And that drinkin' don't help anybody." Benella says she never told anybody that stuff but me. But who knows. He also told Benella that he'd met his real mother, who was light skinned too but rich and that Granddaddy was indeed his real father, and he was going to be a professional musician was why he wasn't going to go to college like everybody said he had to, a pro basketball player maybe, which was why he was taking time off, a singer in Detroit, he said, Motown, he said. Benella says he was always talking big and long about things like that.

Before that, before when some say he was still together and went to visit my mother before I was born, the year my ma was not married and was living alone, that summer in New York, that hot summer in sixty-something right before Raymond was supposed to go to college but wasn't, my mother, who wasn't a mother yet, brought Raymond back home early to Flint, Michigan. Raymond was hearing things. Had James Brown up all the way in the living room with his head right next to the speaker, to drown 'em out, he said. In the middle of the night, chainsmoking, while talking and screaming at folks who weren't there. Waking her sleepover friends with bright flashlight light right in their eyes. My ma had a doctor friend over looking at him, and her friend said Raymond needed help, hospital help.

Story goes, by all accounts save my grandma's, my mother brought Raymond home and told Grandma he was real sick and needed help. Grandma didn't think so. Up until then, that year, that time, that conversation, that was it for talking about something my grandma said she was done talking about. That way of things was the exact reason why my mother says she'd long ago moved far away. The pushiness. The stubbornness. The getting bossed around. My cousin Melvin, who lived with us in New Jersey for a while and then moved down to Atlanta for, he says, some of the very same reasons, so he understands, my cousin Melvin says my mother was grown and had been through college and had put herself through her master's in teaching at the University of Michigan the way both Grandma and Granddaddy had wanted her to but it wasn't enough, the teaching English and living around home. My pop told me one year on the long drive back to New York from Flint, with my mother asleep with her mouth open in the back, "She told your grandma it wasn't enough and her mother said, 'Well, if you think you can do better on your own, you go on ahead and do it,' and so your mother did and moved to New York. She thinks your grandma threw her out and they didn't talk for a while after that."

"And she lived in New York alone, which Mama didn't think proper for a young single woman of marrying age," says my aunt Corine, who I almost always believe 'cause she taught me how to read and write in her basement one summer in Flint when no one else anywhere could. "Your mother," she says, "had seen a great many things and wasn't scared of anything, especially not Mama," she says.

Story goes, she was as smart as anybody black, white, old, or young and knew she was smart like that and I guess decided she wasn't going to knuckle under to anyone but speak her mind to anyone and everyone who needed to hear it in those days and seems there were so many who needed to hear it when my mother tells of those uncomfortable times, being a beautiful six-foot-tall, well-educated black woman always standing out, getting stared at everywhere, sometimes wishing she could blend into the walls being like anyone else. So with Raymond all broken in the head from something she decided she was going to speak her mind to her mother, my grandma, like nobody ever had, like nobody ever did. She spoke up and told her right there early one morning at that long, empty kitchen counter that there was something real wrong with Raymond. Raymond needed help. A New York doctor friend had said so. And a New York doctor certainly knew a lot more than my grandma did.

Lincoln says Grandma didn't care for how she was being spoken to but Lincoln's only a year older than me so he probably wouldn't know. But he says, "It was the tone and the voice and that way of arguing she had, like your mother had raised Raymond, like Raymond was *your* mother's baby," he says it all sure, but how would he know?

Some say Grandma's a spiteful woman. Some say that talk in Flint, that talk with my mother alone at the raised kitchen table, that's the reason why Raymond never saw a doctor. After drinking some, Uncle Otis just says, "Ya grandma's one of those proud, high yella women not used to being told about this or that. Couldn't believe anything she had a hand in, like her Raymond, someone she'd raised and loved, could be crazy or 'sick.' And ya gotta blame somebody for something like that and warn't nobody to blame but ya mama and there ya go."

I myself don't know. I wasn't there. Nobody was there. I asked everybody who might know and a few I knew wouldn't and nothing. Nobody knows. Just speculation and stories, lots and lots of stories, and ever changing lies with everybody spinning and weaving the tale the way they need and want to see it to be.

What I do know is when I was four my mother took me up Broadway for a long while until we came upon a nodding junkie and she said, "This is what happens to the people like your uncle Raymond who do drugs." Another time she broke a plastic bottle of wax over the back of my head for a bad word and cut the waxed tuft out of my hair and next day said she hadn't done it. Stepped off a curb and broke her ankle and still tells people I pushed her. Said nothing when at the beginning of the year I snapped and grabbed her by the throat and lifted and told her to admit it was a big fat fucking lie, me snorting and smoking drugs, along with all the rest she'd heard then said then done. Soon after she wanted all of us to see someone, a family counselor. Things were coming apart and she was afraid of looks in my eye but we'd never been a family to let those sorts of things out to anyone else, lie in the bed you've made, fix your own problems, and so sometimes I wonder about Raymond and the real things nobody knows or maybe does know and just hasn't ever said or done or couldn't do or won't do. Maybe there's much more to the story. Maybe only Raymond and my grandma really know? Maybe just Raymond. Maybe my ma. Maybe just Raymond once knew but his mind's all gone, washed up now so no one will ever know.

But nobody knows any of that stuff about my ma and me and she helped all of her brothers and sisters and nieces and cousins and nephews when they needed her help, wanted to come to New York to stay awhile, needed quiet emergency money, sound stern advice when no one else would or could help them like that and they all love her for it. They all really do. Anyone she helps does. That does something too, so sometimes I think that's why they agree with my mother. Say she tried telling Grandma even Raymond was scared, but Grandma how Grandma is didn't think so, and how they both argued on and on and came to shouting even, with my mother using fancy college words, *schizophrenia* and the such, to show Grandma but how when Grandma is set on something, she doesn't budge, all of them saying how much better she is today than she was back then when my ma was arguing with her and how what my ma says is about right when she says at the end of it all, "Well, he's not my child and it's not my business," which is maybe what a lot of them say to get themselves through.

A lot of folks say if Grandma had gotten Raymond the proper help back then when my mother stood up to her mother, maybe Raymond wouldn't be how he is, crazy. If you ever get folks talking about it for real, folks in the family who were around and remember, and remember the long, slow aftermath, they look off into nothing the way Raymond sometimes does. They get talking full steam and might even get a little angry about it sometimes, a little spiteful about it sometimes, a little teary eyed about it sometimes. "It was that LSD," my mother'll say, she'll say things like, "Drugs and that angel dust and that LSD, I'm sure," she'll say, and "And they could treat that," she'll say on drives back to New York, my father nodding but quiet, "even then," and other folks say things like, "No reason for it, no reason at all, Mama had just budged that once," things like, "It's a shame," things like, "It ain't all her fault, but she coulda done something when she had the chance," things like, "Ain't nothin' nobody can do now," things like, "She gotta lie in the bed she's made," my mother, other folks, say things like that.

Grandma doesn't say anything about it.

"He eat his plate?" Grandma says when she notices me back by the Christmas tree.

"Yes," I say.

"You sit in there with him?"

"Yes," I say.

"What else he say?"

"He said all right," I say, "and he looked like he really liked it," I say.

"And what else?"

"Said he was just going to go to the bathroom and rest for a little while and then he'd come back out soon," and Grandma looks at me and turns and turns back to look at me smiling and then seems to feel better with this. I look away.

DOCTOR TODAY SAYS RAYMOND NEEDS TO STOP DRINKING all the time and he'd get a little better. Stop drinking and live out on his own in a halfway house with a lot of supervision. Grandma doesn't think doctors know much of anything and especially nothing about her Raymond or care the way she cares, and gets to talking about her botched hip and being stuck in that low chair and about her best friend who died under anesthesia 'cause the dentist didn't know black folks turn purple, not red, she always says.

Nobody else knows what to do with her and that's because, I guess, it's not our business, and then what Grandma says is sort of true and not true all at once.

FOOD IS EATEN AND EVERYTHING EVERYWHERE IS DIRTY, and light gospel is coming out over the radio from the living room, where I sit. Hymn sort of thing like something Raymond might've done for Grandma way back when he could still do such things. Piled plates, pots, pans, all about the sink, some still sitting in front of the people still at the table and black Santa Claus–patterned-tablecloth-covered card tables around the house. Raymond is back and up there sweating, with both arms through his coat and laced-up white high tops too tight, head down, quickly finishing his third plate up there at the table, and my grandma shoots me a look. Away from me, my grandma is looking at everybody now, looking the way she gets to looking at Raymond, and already the loud laughing and lying have slowed to half smiles and murmurs. Now stopped, with people feeling Grandma looking and shifting, my relatives now up and moving, snapping pants buttons, buckling belts with excuses and reasons and lies to my grandma, who's now frowning, glaring at them. Raymond grins and clicks and jerks, sweating all over with that jacket, and them headphones blasting, with ash from his smoking cigarette spread about his big belly. He's waiting. Folks up and moving out the door, ignitions being turned over in the driveway and sounds of car engines getting quieter going farther and farther softly over the snow-white-covered road.

Empty.

A quiet about the house except for blaring headphones and Raymond giggling toward the television. It's snowing pretty good outside, the big flakes weighing down all the branches of the evergreens, so they droop down toward the ground. Raymond is looking out the small window, grinning and laughing at something only he sees as my grandma is frowning at him, wanting him to act different and right and not so sick, but how he was supposed to have been. His sneakers are wet and as he jerks they squeak off the metal on the bottom of the stool and I wonder if he's gone out already or is going out soon or maybe even both. My grandma just sits and watches him.

And if you stick around for a spell, don't go too far, maybe take a seat in the big chair in the living room, after a while you'll hear her sigh and say softly, "Oh, Raymond," real quiet, "my baby, my baby," as she rocks up out of her low chair to hobble down the hall to her room to lie down and close her eyes for a real long time.

IMPROMPTU PARADE

THE MAN ON THE SKATEBOARD WITH NO LEGS COULDN'T
see, but the rest of us four deep watched with smiles. With
some it was hard to tell. They all had perfect breasts of
varying incredible sizes, but a bulge gave them away. They
all tried to hide that bulge. They were many in outfits, col-
orfully parading around *Avenida Atlântica*, sliding over
hoods, lying like American pinups in front of tires along
the street, moving in between the halted honking horns,
all of them blowing whistles, licking lips, swishing hips
with heads thrown back to the swaying sounds of Carnaval coming in loud from the *trío eléctrico* two blocks
away. They had a bouncing audience smiling along the
sidewalk and a jeering crowd with heads and fists sticking
out of the windows of the lined-up cars. There was one
as a nun with holes cut away for his massive breasts to
stick out, another as the sparkly winged Tinker Bell, another naked and painted green everywhere he could be,
husky, big and tall up high on his tippy-toes, right in front
of us moving this way and that way like a ballerina,
dandelion flowers littering his hair, with his hands above
his head like a blooming flower, but he had newspaper-
stuff for his breasts and nobody watching let him forget

it. He acted more the part than any of them, though, and everyone there looking pelting him with cruzeiros was sure at this rate by next year he'd have his big breasts, too.

JEANNIE

UP IN THE HILLS, IN THE NIGHT, JEANNIE TURNS OFF the engine, listening to the sound of my voice. She wants to go to the party. With one hand, through the dark, she slowly touches her forehead, the steering wheel, the rearview mirror, my leg, my hair, warm fingers caressing the back of my neck. She looks at me talking and pulls her hand back and rolls down her window, warm air blowing the ends of her hair. It's just rained and it's in the air all through the car. I touch her leg, then her cheek, and remember we're friends. With the back of my hand I touch her cheek again as a friend. We're friends. It's good being friends. She looks at me. I smile. I pause and there's quiet. Drifting music and talking from the party around the corner and she's squirming. She wants to go. I open my window and try talking again. The wind flaps a flag in time with her moving hair. Up the street, through our rain-dripped windshield, the yellow lights of the streetlamps reflect clear like little moons here and there off the many little puddles as the rest of the wet, shiny road sort of glows yellow, off-white. The humid air blowing through the car moves her hair, flaps the flag, as all the moons in the puddles ripple like little waves in a sea. She's squirming again. Jeannie won't ever talk about any of the real bad things and I guess that's why we generally get along.

As I understand it, from what others still say, over at Maplewood Middle, before the big court cases and busings, all the popular pretty white girls started throwing pennies at her 'cause she said things and smoked and drank and was real poor and pretty and a blonde and a Jew. A Jew. A beautiful Jew no one could really figure. Every day wearing all the same clothes, all the time broke but smart and smiling and talking and waving while walking slow to class with her true blond hair and rain-cloud-gray eyes as many would stop and watch her walking while whispering about her doing all the things the good-looking white boys always wanted to do and all the popular, pretty white girls always wanted to do with them but wouldn't do for what they thought everyone would say.

So all day long Maureen Gildea and all the rest of them went around school throwing loads of pennies while smiling and giggling, calling Jeannie a Jew whore and a smiling Jew bitch, Maureen saying to anyone and everyone how Jews always talked your secrets away and couldn't ever, ever be trusted and then how Jeannie liked to spread her legs and do things on her knees with anyone and everyone in the Roman Gourmet bathroom during lunch and in the woods behind the library before school and in the girls' locker room after school sometimes and sometimes even in her mother's king-size bed with two or three of them at a time, letting any and all of them use the same toys her Jew mother, Ms. Shapiro, used on herself, kept in the little red combination-lock suitcase beneath the bed.

After a short while redheaded Dave Williams, whose father was a bigwig policeman and whom Jeannie'll say she liked some, and all the rest of them started every day carrying plastic bags full of pennies and nickels and dimes to school, circling her, then pelting her with handfuls of change, saying loud, "Pick 'em up, pick 'em up, pick 'em up, Jew," laughing, pointing, saying "Jew whore" and "prude bitch" in the halls before and after classes, coughing, "Jew, Jew," while teachers talked in class, bunches of them following her home after school, drinking and laughing and smoking and screaming, "Come on, come on, fucking good-for-nothing Jew bitch," all her long walk home, where they would stay and linger on her lawn, laughing and smiling and screaming, "Let us in, let us in, let us in." It became a thing to do. Something fun, they said.

The neighbors finally started calling the police for the shouting and then her mother got wind of it and her mother's cokehead black boyfriend tried to make some big show of it in the *News Record* paper but suddenly stopped and then her real father came down from Vermont on business and found out and I guess there was some stink about naming all the names which she wouldn't do 'cause she's Jeannie, and then the threats taped on her locker at school from time to time and it sort of went on like that for a while with the school counselor running all around here and there doing a little this and that, trying to make it better but it didn't get better, like these things seldom do.

About February the police and her principal finally figured Jeannie better hurry up and just transfer schools, to our school, where there were other Jewish kids but with money, which they thought more natural and better and easier for everyone involved, and she got there and started every day eating lunch and hanging out with me and

Leonard and Preston, three black guys, 'cause she could feel it, see how those others were, even the other Jews, who wouldn't have anything to do with her.

Five years later, at the beginning of this summer, right after Preston died, all the white ladies in my mother's church group started saying I was going to crash and kill myself too, the way I still zoomed around town in my car like I hadn't learned a thing in the world, and when my soccer coach's wife—who really only repeated what her husband, my coach, said—said the same thing to my mother at one of our summer soccer games, my father shook his head and said, "What can I do, Maceo?" as my mother smiled and talked of lessons saying I'd be walking the rest of the summer no matter where I had to go like I should've been doing all along in the first place. Lessons.

The next week my pop had no choice but to go to this newfangled, cockamamy, rinky-dink drinking and drugging and driving thing for parents at school 'cause of Preston, and when they bought Mrs. Pearlman's story of my snorting things up my nose, which isn't true, coming home saying such things loud in our redbrick driveway in front of my grandma, I began to sweat saying, "You folks don't get it," and "It's not true," as my mother clenched her teeth and her fists and shook screaming, "That's what they said you'd say," and "No son of mine," rushing at me up the long driveway with her open hand raised high how she'll do, as my grandma watched my father saying "Please" as he just looked up at the darkening sky as something inside me gave and slipped and slid and I grabbed my mother midswing and lifted her above my head, her all the while screaming, as I threw her down hard and she's crying there as my father was rushing at me quick now from the car with his hand raised up, him screaming, "No," and "You can't," and "What the . . . ," kind of spitting everything as he tried to say everything, while my grandma said nothing but watched us all from the front door as he went to grab me or push me or something and I slapped his hands and grabbed him around his throat and squeezed and thought I might kill everybody as he held my arms, trying to pull me off, and I looked at him and remembered things and let go and wondered about Preston's head, off slowly rolling with his nose and eyes slapping against the black pavement to bang on some concrete curb while the rest of him flopped and flipped down Vauxhall Road with his twisting, twirling big blue '76 Chevy Impala. Nobody can say how it happened.

My parents sent my grandma back early to California with my aunts, who don't have any kids. My mother still won't talk to me much but will tell all those white ladies in her church group how people make mistakes and change and deserve second, third, and fourth chances and turn the other cheek and he who has not sinned and all that jazz, but that's a different story, I say to Jeannie, and doesn't seem to apply much to me or anyone I know.

"I don't get it," she says.

Most times I try to say things but it doesn't come out right. Most times Jeannie seems to know and just understand and I guess that's why we generally get along. These are all the things I was thinking and hoping to remind Jeannie of without really saying any of it for real while she sat looking at me and sometimes touching me as a friend along with all the other things all around her car while she squirmed with the windows open in the dark beneath the tree with the warm wind blowing her hair and the moons up the wet and glowing road.

"I don't get it," she says again, "but you two don't treat your mother right I know that," she says.

"It's a different story," I say as she looks out the water-dripped windshield as the flag starts flapping quickly and her hair moves as if we're driving fast. "She says things," I say. "She says things, then she does things, and it's not so nice," I say.

The drifting talking and bad music from around the corner from the party and some metal clanging against the flagpole and magazines in her backseat ruffling loud.

"Well," I say, "so you see what I mean?" I say.

"No," she says, "I don't," she says, "I don't know what that has to do with anything."

"No?" I say. "Well," I say.

"I don't know why we're talking about any of this. I mean, what does any of this change?" she says.

"Well," I say, and then she says nothing, and "But you know," I say as her hair hides her face, then gives it to me full, "everyone in there is shit," I say, "and has done things," I say, and she touches my leg and puts her hand in my hair and warm fingers all around the back of my neck, like friends.

"We'll just leave if it's no good," she says.

"I know," I say.

"It's a party," she says, "a party," she says, "we can just leave," she says, "a party with people at a house," she says, "lots of people we don't know," she says, "and we don't have to drink, and we can just look and leave if it's no fun, 'cause you can't hide forever," she says, looking out the window as a piece of her hair in my hair lightly touches the tip of my ear, now my mouth. I scratch and grab and can't see it, can't get it. The wind, the hair, my ear, then my mouth like that.

"Yeah," I say, and she smiles at me and looks away and starts the car, headlamps off the puddles and street, her hair blowing straight back as she goes slow, then fast, with two hands on the wheel, splashing puddles to turn right around the corner to slow and stop and we get out to a big, lighted house with white people moving here and there across all the big, opened windows, past the shadows of people I don't know sitting cross-legged in small circles in the dark, smoking cigarettes on the lawn, looking at us and waving and smiling, "Hello," one of them says, turning and talking and smoking like before, up and there's a couple I can't see well, kissing, touching, moving, making out not so high in a big oak tree. He has her shirt off and his moving hands disappearing in and out of leaf shadows and her unbuttoned pants.

Inside white people everywhere, mud on the white carpet, red keg cups sitting on everything, with people moving all around, laughing and drinking and smoking and talking loud in all the many rooms as music plays, Def Leppard, and a pack of girls singing along loud, knowing all the words, air guitar, hand to mouth like a mike, in the sunroom, where J.D.'s father has his antique Civil War guns and big-game heads all over the wall, and movement, people with drinks moving, all around the house, people looking at us and coming over and stopping us, saying "Nice to see you out" and "Sorry, sorry, sorry about Preston, I heard about Preston" and "Terrible about Preston" and "Do you think you'll start next year at Dartmouth?" pointing us over there for the keg, outside through the big glass doors to the outside bar for hard drinks, pretty girls with feathered hair, puffed perms, pretty going down and up the winding staircase as Maureen Gildea, smiling, comes over, giving a big hug to Jeannie, who smiles back, and "Sorry about Preston," she says, "it's really terrible," she says, "we've all been so sad," she says, and then "Downstairs," they all say with a wink, "for the other things if you're interested," and quickly they all disappear away through the people, people, to some place, someone else.

Jeannie says she'll get us a beer if I want and she smiles and I smile back, and "I'll be over here," I say as I walk some and smell the reefer rising from the basement and walk some more past people, people, people, following Pat McNeely, the linebacker for the football team, pushing holes through the crowds of people in the long, narrow hallway standing and talking loud over the Def Leppard piped all through the house, and I look left over some shoulders at the door and Leonard is sitting in a brown La-Z-Boy with his feet up next to a fan with the heads of his green Heineken bottles sticking out of his little cooler packed with ice he takes to all the parties now.

A bunch of folks I don't know are playing Nintendo and turn and see me, and "We're sorry, man, we heard," each one nodding, me not noticing which one of them has said it as Leonard looks at them and shakes his head, and "Two ways to deal with it, really," raising his nearly finished beer to me, and "Good to see you out," he says.

"I told you we were coming," I say.

"You say a lot of things," he says, tipping his head and beer all the way back to get it all, get it all, now looking at me, "Who's we?" he says.

"Me and Jeannie."

And he smiles and looks out the opened window through the spinning fan cutting everything slow, then back to me, "Right where Preston left off, huh?" and he looks down, "Real classy," he says, "class move," he says, "You two been fuckin'," he says, "that what took you so long?"

"We're friends," I say.

"Yeah," he says, "great friends," he says, looking down, shaking his head, "fuck friends," he says to the floor, over the Def Leppard and bleeping Nintendo football and people everywhere drunk, loud talking, loud laughing, screaming, girls shrieking. Leonard doesn't look up for a while and then reaches into his cooler for another beer. He opens it with his teeth.

"Where's the bitch, anyway?" he says.

"Hey."

"Four days," he says, "I'm all for fuckin', and you know that, too, fuck two, three at the same time, I don't care, one of these dumb girls round here, all right, shit, I wouldn't care if you fucked some old saggy forty-year-old house-wife, even nasty Ms. Wastpee, I'd say all right. I would've, too, I had the chance, but this shit, man this shit is wrong all over. Three ways to handle this and you've chosen the two worst. Shoulda just been coming out with me to the city, get twisted up in them cheap bars I know."

"Well, you know everything, man, no fucking telling you anything, 'cause you don't listen."

"Yeah," he says, "that's right," he says, and lets down his legs, "and I don't fuck my boy's—check that, my dead boy's old lady," he says as the four playing football start jumping up and down. A touchdown. Leonard looks at them and waves me over and the light hitting the blades of the fan in the window makes it look slow, like I can put my hand through and not get cut.

"Those fucks punched out the Domino's guy," he says, "Jimmy Lowell."

"No!"

"Those fucks," he says. "That Kevin Greeley. All of 'em there, all cranked up doing that shit, forget who they're fucking with, and you know he's coming back. He'll be back with a whole bunch of them Newark cats looking to whoop some ass, jack folks up baseball bat bad."

"Fuck."

"They see him coming and start snickering and he's trying to play it all cool and they say, 'Nigger, we're not going to pay,' and he says, 'All right,' and just turns and starts walking back to his car, big Jimmy Lowell, you know, and then that J.D. says, 'We still want the pies,' and Jimmy keeps walking toward his car and Pat McNeely runs out there screaming, 'Nigger,' and there's a few watching, you know, those girls, so you know how he gets, and he jumps on him and then they all were on, like five of 'em, kicking and punching, knocking the shit outta him, his nose, maybe his jaw, lots of blood," he says, "lots of blood and then they go in his car and take all the other pies and leave him there and you know he's gonna come back soon, they're all fucked up," he says.

"We need to go," I say.

"Yeah, yeah right, we need to go," he says, finishing his beer again, "I was just waiting for you to come, 'cause I didn't want you coming here getting caught in all this shit, but you didn't say you were coming with the bitch— where is she, anyway?" he says. " 'Cause they're coming back and most folks didn't see it and those idiots are too fucked up to realize. That was some time ago, so I figure just enough time to clean up and get real, real mad and call a whole bunch of ass-kickin' black brothers."

"We need to go," I say.

"Where's Preston's bitch?" he says.

"Hey, man, enough of that," I say.

"What the fuck is wrong with you?" Leonard says.

"That girl," he says, "You know it was that girl," he says.

"Well," I say, "we're just friends," I say.

"Yeah," he says, "well, go find your friend," he says as the four jump up screaming again and the fat one yanks a cord or something and the screen goes blank, then blue, and now they're yelling at the fat kid, who's laughing, and Leonard looks at me, then the ground, shaking his head, "Real classy," he says, "go find your classy girl," he says, closing his cooler, "I'm getting the hell outta here. You can come with me if you want, but . . ." he says, getting up as I sit down and look at him moving toward the door as the four freshmen have started a new game and the fat one is playing now, but looking through the fan outside at the people laughing and drinking and smoking and moving but all cut up, for the blade's moving so fast it's slow in the light.

Out in the hall through the people, and people laughing, watching some guy up on the balcony load up the beer funnel as another one plugs up the bottom with his thumb and now he's doing it, cheeks all puffed and wide, back through the doors and through the laughing people and now it's Quiet Riot or something and everyone is fucked up and singing this trash too and pushing past people, past the jumping long line for the bathroom as two people I don't know are banging on the door, and up the stairs and all the rooms are locked and I knock on all the doors and there's no answer and back down the spiraling stairs and out the front and Leonard's car is gone but the couple is still up in the tree, hands moving all over each other through the leaf shadows and inside and through people, people, screaming, talking, touching one another, playing quarters on J.D.'s mother's mahogany dining-room table, brown mud sneaker treads all over the beige carpet, all over the house, and downstairs to the basement through the thick reefer smoke in the narrow staircase to slow and peer down through a dim light at the fucks sitting on a black leather couch around a table with a bong and maybe a spoon and some other things I can't make out, many red eyes looking up at me, and back up the stairs through the loud people, pushing loud people, screaming people, past the long, jumping-up-and-down bathroom line, where the same two are banging, banging on the door.

I lean next to the hanging baby-blue phone. A rotary one. Eight Domino's boxes sit half-opened on the floor and kitchen chairs and glass table with crusts and half-eaten pizza. "Fucks," I say, looking out into the backyard through the opened glass door, and people in shorts and tanks and white skin moving, moving all over, leaning in, talking to one another, perfect white teeth smiling and grinning, big red cups tipped in mouths, tiki torch flames all over as far back and wide as I can see.

"Thank God," and "I was gonna piss myself," and "Oh lookit," and I turn left and redheaded Dave Williams walks out of the bathroom, wiping his mouth, turning around, tucking the back of his shirt in, saying loud, "Guy's gotta do," as people come running into the kitchen screaming and I look back over to the bathroom and J.D. comes out smiling and all the guys start smiling and all the girls sorta frown as Jeannie walks out of the bathroom, wiping her mouth, putting an earring in.

Redheaded Dave Williams and J.D. look over at me and smile at each other and then me and sorta shrug and walk the other way, then downstairs.

She sees me and bows her head and starts walking over toward me. All the screaming, smiling people look at her coming and at me and go back outside quickly quiet. She's in the kitchen and she stops and looks up at me with red eyes and then back down. I put my hand on the wall. My hands are sweating. I'm sweating. I walk over to the opened glass door then grab hold of a cabinet and open the cabinet door and I'm sweating all over and back to the phone and she hasn't moved. She comes over to me with hands out, her hands starting around my waist, and I push her away and I'm sweating, sweating, everything is sweating, my arms and my legs sweating, and she comes again with hands out near the phone and I think of her with her hand on her mouth, think of her doing things, doing things, doing things in the bathroom with those fucks, doing things, and it goes soft and starts slipping and she's cringing beneath the baby-blue phone as my hand is up high and I'm screaming and she's cringing and I swing, hard and fast, and she freezes with a small hand over her ear, eyes closed tight, and I'm screaming things and knock the baby-blue phone above her off its cradle, so it rings as it slips down and bangs on the red tiled floor.

She's crying and goes and sits down and I'm still screaming and walk over to her and she's cringing and I walk back to where they've stopped playing quarters but are watching and people on my back and the mahogany table is collapsing as there are two of them kicking, punching, stomping on me as I try to get up, and a foot in the eye and people are screaming and redheaded Dave Williams is screaming "Nigger" with his mouth open wide, "Always wanted to do this," he's saying as J.D. is kicking my belly and Kevin Greeley has a knee in my back, smacking my face, ears, and I can't move and roll up in a tight ball and they stop as I'm stretched out on my stomach and blood in my nose and mouth and the whole house is screaming and the thud-thump of many running feet as I lie with my eyes closed, face in the beige carpet, her body warm next to mine, her hand on my cheek as I groan, thinking of Preston's head off and slowly rolling to bang softly against the concrete curb, his one half-battered eye up and watching me like he knew the whole time.

PRINCESS

WITH A FLASH IN THE RAIN I TOOK THEIR SMILING PIC-
ture in front of their shopping cart filled with the crushed,
wet cans they'd been picking up around the parade all
day, when Hans leaned over and took the younger sister
by the hand, snaking her slowly through the dancing
crowd toward the bleachers loaded with drenched people
moving to the samba drums beating down the street. The
grandma smiled and the mother did, too, and I tried hoping they didn't know what they were doing, though they
gave their youngest a soggy blanket from the bottom of
the cart. Public places had become his new little parade
thing. I waited, watching his blond hair through the sea of
rolling brown; rain on the puddles and shiny arms, on the
thin, wet clothes now see-through and sticking to the
moving, wet bodies, when a hand on my hand turning me,
so I turned to see the fat older sister smiling, jiggling in
the rain to the banging beat rolling down the avenue. She
couldn't have been more than fourteen, with that see-
through shirt revealing two dark brown nubs no different
from some fat little boy's. PRINCESS in silver it said in little letters across the wiggling chest. And though the *bloco*
passed us, with the crowd going crazy now, with many
there in the street dancing along and behind them, she

faced only me, sambaing up on toes, hips and pelvis working around to the sounds, shaking, shifting, bending, slapping her big ass, never, not once, taking her eyes off of me
as her mother winked at her daughter in the rain and then
at me, and the grandma smiled with a hand tight on the
cart, nodding at me, rubbing the granddaughter's moving
shoulders and big ass as the dancing daughter kept trying
to draw me in by pulling on the camera around my neck,
rubbing her wet legs and ass, all the while saying in rhythm
and time, "Beautiful smile, boxing shoulders," and "Boxing smile, beautiful shoulders," smiling and smiling, so I
couldn't take it and had to turn and walk away.

LIGHTHOUSE

BENEATH THE BLUE BLANKETS OF THE MOTEL BED WE lie naked, not touching, not moving in the shifting shadows of the blue white TV glow, beer bottles, towels, guidebooks, flip-flops, underwear, clothes, scattered all around the moving corners of the room. Baseball game down low so I can hardly hear, blue blankets bunched up on her waist, bare back turned at me, glimpse of breast, "You awake?" I say softly, May's one foot sticking out of the covers at the bottom of the bed. "Hurt still?" I say a little louder, everything flickering light then dark, the full bottled Corona she used still leaning on her thigh catching all the lights. "You awake?" I say louder, her long brown hair spreading over her shoulders flat and wide in the narrow space between us. "Does it hurt?" running my palm close and slow and not touching all down and over the long swell of her body and back up and down again slow so I can still feel the warm of her skin through the cool air of the AC like before. Again I want to lick the salt off of her skin, touch the lines of her face and long legs and nipples like dimes but nothing. I close my eyes and roll on my back, concentrating over again. Trying to see her. See May. Moving and sweating beneath the white sheet. White sheet bobbing. Bedspread on the floor. Her wet mouth working.

Soft hands holding, fumbling, stroking, struggling to make something out of nothing. Concentrating but nothing. Nothing. I open my eyes.

"Hot?"

"Pissed?"

"Pretending," I say, turning the volume all the way up on the game, crowd cheering, announcers talking heavy and loud all throughout our room and nothing and shaking the bed a little so she shakes a little in the baseball noise and nothing and "Your pants were at your ankles," I say through the noise, turning off the TV but nothing, "It looked funny," I say with everywhere the sour smell of unfinished warm beer and dark and quiet. Quiet.

The purr of the air conditioner and loud talking of the big fireworks through the wall behind my head. Big, heavy footsteps from above and the blinking neon red cowboy on his red neon horse motel sign through our thin shade reflecting big and fat and pink on the leaning Corona then nothing and fat and big and pink then nothing and ruby red off the side of her shiny brown hair then nothing and neon red on her five toes painted dark and glossy then nothing. A car horn and a long, low American car horn and some drunk screaming, "Shelllllllllllly," loud from somewhere close and "Yes, Shelllllllllly, ohhh," again and some laughing from some place else and me getting out of bed and pulling the shade over to the side a little looking for the something, seeing nothing, now watching the few straggling cars from the Fourth of July traffic going through town. All of them slow at the blinking yellow light and through and fast off into the distance till just tiny bits of red lights small against the looming, dark mountains, thinking of my best friend, Lee, shaking his head, telling me I was going to do something with May. "You're going to do something," flat and plain he said over a beer at the bar back in the beginning in New York. "Just don't lie to yourself," he said, "all alone for that amount of time? How you two get? How you two get when no one's there to stop you?" and "What," I said, and "Just some time away," he said, "what bullshit!" He smiled. "Just some time away! What's Kendra say?" and "About what?" I said as he grinned down at the silver bar, not looking at me, saying out loud what my girlfriend, Kendra, thought and always wanted to say but wouldn't 'cause she really wants it to work and sometimes saying something makes it not work, and the neon red cowboy and horse in my eyes and pulling the shade back down and watching May through the moment of dark and then red light.

Watching her shoulder, her cheek, her little nipples, then nothing and "One bed," May said to the motel guy, pulling in before the cowboy was all lit up, "Cheaper that way," she said, "it'll be good," she said, looking at me sure, "The cheapest ya got," she said, "Things'll last longer," she said, and I smiled 'cause she seemed to be happy and smiling and the motel guy was smiling and for a few moments I thought the last times in the other hotels with May might slip away, dissolve, disappear into nothing so these times could feel exciting like the first times, fresh and new and wrong and right again, so I smiled and put my hand on her lower back like lovers do and she smiled back and brushed up close like lovers do, and the whir of the many air conditioners up and down the rows of rooms and long lines of her legs beneath the blue blanket then nothing. Firecrackers pop-popping close and one big boom echoing long through the desert valley from some place far and her curled and naked and unmoving in the blinking, soft red light, thin lipped, cold, pale, then nothing and pink, peaceful, clean then nothing.

"It looked funny, is all," I say softly in the blinking dark, thinking of her by the side of the desert road jumping up barefoot, kicking her lawn chair over into a drunk Weeble-wobble dance, her hopping and stopping and hopping and smacking her leg once, then twice, pulling her shorts to her ankles, no underwear, flash of ass, her squatting next to our car like an inky ball, is what she looked like, an inky ball in that desert blue black light from the shadows, from the silhouettes of the many faraway dark mountains, her saying soft, "Something bit me," and me drinking my cold Corona, trying not to laugh anymore. Not to laugh looking at her nearly naked there like a big, inky blue black tumbleweed of a ball as the Fourth of July traffic stood stopped, lined up, so all the red brake lights looked like a red river running all the way down the hill to the shifting red and white car lights in the Scorpions' high school parking lot, right next to the Scorpions' football field, where the little white flashlights moved here and there, 'cause that's where they were gonna set off the fireworks from, as the guy at our motel counter said, "Go early and stay high and you'll be like a local," he said, so we got there when the air was hot and dry before the sun went down, when you could still see the pastel pinks and greens and baby blues and desert reds and browns and oranges in the faraway buttes and mountains, and we started drinking and drinking and forgetting the heavy things, smiling and laughing at the silly things, eating bar-becue chicken and burgers and hot dogs, drinking beer with all the strangely friendly redneck locals all up and down the sides of the two-lane road until good and late, when you could see only pieces of moving people by the light of their barbecue grills. We sat down in our lawn chairs so we could sit for a while and rest and drink and wait for the fireworks. Waiting while watching all the headlights from the many cars making all the yellow reflectors and white glass in the road glimmer and sparkle and shine and she jumped up saying, "Ohhh," wobbling her chair, doing that hopping and stopping business as I was drinking my beer and she with her ass out squatting looking like a big, tumbly, inky blue black ball by the Jeep near a cactus and that's when I said, "What, did a scorpion get ya?" laughing and drinking and she didn't move but was in that ball in the shadows with her blowing hair and I said, "What, did a scorpion get ya or something?" louder 'cause those were the things that used to make May smile but she didn't. Came over and looked at me and started right there with that silent treatment just like my Kendra likes to do and that's when May leaned down and grabbed a full Corona from the cooler, sat in the truck, put the cold beer on her leg, slammed the door, closed her eyes, leaned the seat all the way back so I couldn't see her anymore and the whir of the AC and the heavy footsteps from the room above and "It looked funny, is all," I say again as the blinking red cowboy gives me her shoulder, her face, the two lines of her legs beneath the blue blanket, and on the Corona big and fat and pink and then nothing.

With her eyes closed, in that half-light, I can see the high cheeks of her mother, the small chin like her sister's, her puffed-out lips how Kendra always likes to sleep. Almost like sisters. It makes me wonder what I once saw in the one and am now losing in the other.

Crawling in bed, beneath the covers, close but not touching, smelling her skin and smoky barbecue hair, as the heavy footsteps walk and stop and a shower from one of the rooms somewhere, and I lean over so my chest is touching her bare back and lift the warm Corona bottle, slowly, holding the warm, long neck between my finger and thumb.

"What are you doing!" she says, sitting up quickly, blankets moving, body skimming mine, breasts, belly, arms, out from the blanket then nothing and looking at me in the red light with gray eyes waiting, waiting, sweat between her small breasts, then nothing. "What are you doing?" she says louder.

"You're awake," I say.

"You're a little boy," she says.

"I knew you were awake," I say.

"I'm dehydrated," she says, licking her lips. "Give it back," she says.

"We missed the fireworks," I say.

"Stop the bullshit," she says.

"It's warm."

"Then get me a cold one."

"Drank 'em while you were pretending to be pissed."

"I am pissed."

"Well, what do ya do with that?" I say.

"It's what you don't do that really does it," she says.

"I do the best I can with what I got."

"Yeah," she says, "is that what you say to all the girls you do this to?"

"Nope, just you," I say, " 'cause you're so special," I say.

"Yeah," May says, "I feel so very special, I feel great," she says, "I felt great twice in Colorado," swishing her bare leg out from under the blankets, "and super once in Nebraska, and just wonderfully special right before that, a whopping new *Guinness Book of World Records* record three nights in a row across Kansas, remember? And here I am again," she says, looking down in the dark, rubbing her thigh a little and the soft red light with her head down touching the spot then dark and nothing.

"Swollen, see?" she says. "See the two holes where whatever got me got me?" she says. "See?" as she rubs her swollen leg.

"It's a little swollen."

"How 'bout that bottle back, Ace?"

"It's a little swollen," I say again, looking at her naked, long leg and nothing, now touching the little swollen part with my finger where she got bitten by something and "Let's get you some ice or something," I say.

"Yeah," she says.

"Front desk'll have it."

"They don't."

"How 'bout the gas station?"

"Only place open is the Wal-Mart."

"Well, all right," I say.

"It's fifty miles away," she says.

"And warm beer bottles make scorpion and other voodoo bump-in-the-night bug bites fly right away," I say. "We'll bring the cooler and it'll be an adventure and I'll get some Tums," I say, " 'cause God knows I need something," I say, and she jumps up putting on her shorts without underwear and her breasts shaking a little in the red light then nothing and out the door and down to the car, me following, and a burst of dry heat all around me now locking the motel door in the hum of the ACs up and down the rows of rooms and in the car and off.

At the blinking yellow light I slow and she looks at me and then out her window toward the dark mountains. I move some of her hair off her forehead, out of her eyes, and "I'm sorry about your leg and laughing and making fun," I say, "I just didn't think you'd get that pissed about it," I say.

"You're such a fool," she says, "that's what you really think?" she says. "You really believe I'd get naked and kiss you and do those things for you being pissed?" she says. "You really think I'd be fine one minute doing those things for you and then suddenly mad again so I didn't want to?" she says.

"I don't know," I say. "Well," I say, "it's difficult to explain, I guess, with only one condom, sometimes I get nervous and don't wanna get really goin'," I say, " 'cause, you know. People get pregnant," I say, "and then what, 'cause—"

"Yeah," she says, "so with two condoms things would've been fine with you?" she says. "Two condoms in Kansas and things would've gone right up and on forever with you?" she says. " 'Cause I can get boxes of condoms," she says, "I can get boxes and boxes if that'll do it, why, I bet they sell condoms right here in Arizona, at gas stations and bars, maybe even at the Wal-Mart," she says, " 'cause they sell them everywhere, you know, even in Guam, if you know how to look."

"Yeah," I say.

"Yeah," she says.

"Yeah," I say as I look both ways and accelerate through the yellow light, high beams on, moving farther and farther away from the blinking red cowboy on his horse and the few city lights in my rearview mirror till there is nothing but black all around except our brights illuminating the yellow reflectors and sparkling white glass and small parts of the giant mountains and quickly passing electric poles over to her side. No cars pass us either way. It's late now.

"Let's open all the windows," she finally says, opening the moon roof. And we do.

Warm desert air going all through the car, making me have to lick my lips and relick my lips as she puts on Carmex, and I turn off all the interior lights making everything as dark inside as out, so it's hard to see her. "Perfect," she says nicely, and I realize, I now see this is what she does, this softer tone of hers, as I try to ignore her and look at the road and up at millions of stars framed by the moon roof, and like that for a long while with no radio on but the sparkling road and mountains and poles and wind blowing loud in from the night.

"And do you see that?" she says.

"No," I say, "I'm driving."

"See?"

"No."

"Pull over," she says, and so I stop in the middle of the road leaving the car engine running because there won't be any cars, sure, but you never can tell. We get out and "Listen," she says, "turn off the car," she says, and so then I do 'cause this is what I do and "Get the lawn chairs," she says soft, looking out at something, and I do. We put our lawn chairs in the middle of the flat, long road facing the same way and it makes me nervous. "Look," she says, "here it comes," and way out across the darkness like a spinning lighthouse light a small, tight beam shines across the desert plains but does not reach us or the mountains, dies somewhere out in the dark I can't make out.

"What is that?" she says with her nice voice.

"For the planes or something," I say.

"Out here?"

"Army planes, maybe?" I say.

"Looks like a desert lighthouse," she says in the almost quiet.

Stars.

"Listen," she says.

"The cicadas?"

"Listen," she says, and I listen harder and now hear the low hum from the black wires stretching across the electric poles going as far forward and back as I can see from the middle of the road in this dark.

"How's your leg?" I say.

"What happens to you?" she says.

"I'm not sure," I say.

"Do you ever do this with Kendra?"

"What?" I say.

"What you can't do," she says, "or won't do," she says.

"No," I say.

"Anyone else?" she says.

"Who else?" I say.

"Don't you still like me?"

"I like you."

"So, what are you doing?"

"With what?"

"Then, you still want this?"

"I think you're beautiful."

"It's selfish, really, what you do to me, what you do and say," she says.

"It's not so much about being selfish or not being selfish. I think about it."

"Yeah," she says, "yeah, then why do you do this to us?" she says. "To me?" she says a little harder.

" 'Cause you're selfish," she says, "a selfish coward bastard," she says soft again, "it doesn't work that way, if nobody's told you yet, not with me, anyway, and I don't care what she says or thinks but if you're with me you're going to have to—"

"I just get thinking and everything gets jammed up and I try to put everything out of my mind, all of it, and try thinking about you and the great time we're having and how good it feels and you're beautiful and how good it feels to be with someone beautiful and I think of that and the great time we're having and I look and you've started with the things you know I really, really like and I don't have a condom but I close my eyes 'cause things are going pretty good and then something I can't figure happens in my mind and things start coming at me so fast I can't stop it and I'm thinking about everything and I look down and it's all jammed all over again and I know you'll be real upset and pissed and I try but it won't go no matter what I try and then it's all shitty. That's what happens. It's not selfish. It's not really you so much either. Sometimes I think it's—"

"Shhhh," she says, "you should try not thinking so

much," she says, "it isn't about thinking," she says, "these things aren't about thinking at all, just enjoying the time right now, how it feels," she says.

"Shhhh," she says, "don't talk," she says, "just listen and look around. It's so beautiful and quiet here. Feel how nice the air out here is this time of night. Who would think. All the stars and the air and that light. What do you think that is?" she says as the light slowly comes across, quickly breaking the blackness and then nothing, and "We've still got some trip ahead of us," she says. "If you're patient and work hard and let the right stuff flow, the bad things come and happen and move on. If you're calm and patient and don't worry and don't get too upset and just keep going, you'll see, the bad will just pass right along and the good will come right behind it and work itself out. You'll see," she says, "it's true," she says, looking up at the night, "it's true," she says again, looking out the other way up the road as the never-ending low hum of the electric wires blends in with the purr of the cicadas and some of the other desert things making noises while moving around in the flash of the sometimes broken black night.

ILHA DE ITAPARICA

WITH THE KEYS IN THE IGNITION OUR HOT TAXI STOOD dead still in the heat by the side of the road. The new road was just paved and jet black. It smelled of tar and was shimmering like water outside the open van door. Out the back window it shimmered in the sun all the way down as far as you could see with cactus greens and desert browns off to its sides. The one road of the island connecting the palm trees of the coasts. My sweet Ada had her eyes closed, frowning and fanning herself next to me, sweating all over her face and back while holding her curly black hair up off of her neck, hoping to catch some of the warm puffs of air coming through the door. Next to me I could feel her sweat and heat. Looking at her beautiful and sweating, it was hard not to touch her but one must bide his time.

So I leaned forward and like her closed my eyes, hoping for the little wind while listening to the sweat rolling down my face, off my chin, to tip-tap onto the floor, and then to the tar breeze blowing from time to time through the open door. Jangling his keys, moving his loose papers around the hot van, our light-skinned, roly-poly taxi driver was yakking it up all the while right there on a wooden stool in the warm shade of the little shack bar, drinking big *cervejas* and talking loud, telling stories and then laughing hard, listening to the few others in there spinning them, too. They sounded like pirates when they laughed. That we had to catch the last ferry off Ilha de Itaparica meant nothing. "Big trip," he'd said, smoking and sweating while hot and driving through the burning sun of the middle of nowhere, "need more passengers," in English, looking back at Ada hungrily for a second time as the tiny van kicked up dust, slowing down, moving over to the side of the road. "We have to catch a ferry," Ada had shouted out the window as he walked away from us past the rusty, locked petrol pump toward the stools of the thatched-roof bar. You didn't need to speak Portuguese not to like him.

We were there a long time baking and sweating and then something on the wind and I opened my eyes and out the back window as far as I could see into the shimmering a large whiteness moving and filling the road, a growing white river of black bodies dressed all in white, moving slowly out of the shimmering water, shaking tall white signs, and chanting something you could hear faintly when the wind blew right. I shook Ada, who opened her eyes out of sleep to turn and see the procession of chanting children and women with heads bowed holding up pictures of Jesus and of a smiling teenage girl on signs and big snapshots above their heads with some men of the cloth on both sides of the moving whiteness holding wooden white crosses on tall sticks, marching solemnly with big voices leading the chanting prayers in call and response. The procession grew while getting closer so you could see the folds of their clothes and the two dark women out in front of it all, one older, one younger, holding each other, crying and looking up to the sky, shrieking with fists and grief. The procession seemed to be coming out of nothing going on forever and I couldn't help but wonder where so many people on such a small island had come from to go so far into the heat of the middle of nowhere. The demonstration got louder and closer and the two wailing women in front, hands up and open, reaching for something in the air beyond their grasp, now screaming at the blue of the cloudless sky could be heard above the chanting, above everything, even the laughing pirates in the warm shade of the bar. Ada looked out and then leaned over me, her breast touching my leg and slid the van door shut. She rolled the windows up and the heat but I didn't say anything.

Our taxi driver came out of the thatched-roof bar. He passed the locked petrol pump and then us in his van without notice, heading directly for the shimmering road. He put his hand above his eyes and walked some toward the nearing procession. He stopped and squeezed his eyes and the demonstration froze, made no sounds. He squeezed his eyes and the wailing women took two steps forward and for a second nothing in the world moved. The black-mustached taxi driver grinned and, tilting his head back, put his big *cerveja* bottle to his lips. He wiped his mouth, wiped his mouth, took a step forward, and grinned, saying bad things in Portuguese with the hands going to match.

He said many things and then turned to make a run for it. Ada leaned, with her sweaty body sliding over mine, and began locking the doors. The man was very fat and not fast but was at his van quickly, trying the last locked door. His door. He looked at us. Like a lady, Ada sat up and straightened her back and looked into his face. He tried the handle again hard, shaking the tiny van, and I turned my head the other way.

The man was very fat and not fast but tried to make a run for it up the shimmering road but like that the white river swarmed him, kicking and punching, swinging wildly as the big wooden signs with the pictures of the girl soared up, then down, in big arcs. Many white wooden crosses lay over in the dust of the side. The river was on him, yelling and shrieking and growling, and he swung and kicked some trying to stay standing, bending, trying to fight and push through them but there were many grabbing hands and soon he came crashing down cursing, coughing, and screaming 'cause they had him, little feet stomping him from all over, little hands smashing his big head on the ground. The swing of the signs, the crack of wood on bone, and sweet Ada opening the big sliding door to let in some of the cool breeze over my sweat.

A siren coming fast with a flashing red-and-blue light going around and around, two men with badges and long wooden sticks and silver-buttoned blue uniforms making their way through the muttering river of white. The *policía* pulled something from the middle of the people that looked very much like our taxi driver but it was hard to tell.

Some of the men in the thatched bar had come out, *cerveja* in hand, to watch the show and one went with a blue handkerchief and wiped some blood off his big face but then just turned around, sipping his beer, passing the rusted red and locked petrol pump on his way to the stools in the shade.

The *policía* stood over our not-moving van driver as the two women began to wail and embrace again as the demonstration without the tall signs now slowly emerged behind them. We all watched until the river faded into the trembling road. The *policía* turned and looked at the fat thing, sprawled, motionless, face flat in the dust near some of the broken white signs with ripped pictures. They put handcuffs on him to be sure. They dragged him prone through the heat and stuffed him into the back of their squad car. The small car gave with his weight but he didn't move. They drove slowly and didn't put on their siren or flash their red-and-blue light. Coming toward us, one of them looked into the backseat and then turned around, smiling, giving his partner a soft elbow.

"You drive," Ada said to me, moving up to the front.

UPTOWN

UPTOWN.

High above the wide street, polished silver subways floating over invisible rails roar along like long beams of light, screeching, swaying, rumbling, rattling into car horns and bus brakes and laughing by shirtless old men out sweating under warm tree shadows on milk crates and metal chairs playing dominoes and drinking beer while barbecuing and shit-talking over truck engines and car horns with the sidewalk shivering some with the grumbling and growling and screeching and swaying and rattling and roaring over invisible rails like polished beams of silver out of the old uptown station through the early evening heat like some subway has done for as long as anyone around remembers.

Down below she liked to sit and watch the trains.

When the weather was good and cool and we were still pretending, she'd sit alone on a stoop across from the many tall projects along the wide, busy street, looking and listening while waiting and watching for me to come home from work. That was right when the first of the protests started over the eviction of an old man named Dominguez paying two hundred bucks a month, not able to afford ten times that. Right when she still tried to sit close to be close and wore what she knew I liked to see her wear, in a light sundress out on her stoop next to me softly, holding my hand, caressing my ear, pointing and talking of all the beautiful things she'd seen all day like she used to do in the beginning, downtown, back when things were good and new and no one had to fake it. But with this summer heat she'd given all that up. "Too hot," she said back on that smoldering smog-alert day, "awful air," she said with that fake accent, walking the little ways into the brand-new, shiny, air-conditioned café where all the brand-new, hip white folks liked to go, Kendra sitting with her gaze gently drifting through the window about the neighborhood here, now there, this way and that way, up then down, at the lost people chasing after the fast-moving things, her without a word watching and dreaming with her long beige legs stretched out and crossed and her eyes softly slipping up and over the passing silver trains.

Now, hot and off the train and through the dirty heat down the escalator past the cops in the cop car to stand and watch the red light. Another train roars above and I watch the wheels and near me on a scaffolding four Yugoslavs in yellow rain suits spray-cleaning the newly bought building not paying attention but mouth open watching the small and loud conga circle of protesting Puerto Ricans across the street. People pass by the beat cop and Day-Glo protest signs leaning against the gutted picture-frame shop now up for lease, while an older woman, maybe forty with long hair and a red flamenco dress, swishes her hiked-up skirt, and her sweating and clapping and twirling and stomping to the rhythms of the nodding men banging out the heavy Afro beats. A blond dreadlocked white boy in a dashiki now sitting on a crate with a conga. A spectacle. A festival. A vaudeville show. Flamenco dancing. Here. Her head held high. Strained face. Muscled calves, her hands, that dress. Jesus. Moving over by the drummers and leaning in and touching the young white boy tender across the face, but I turn my head like I often do, for what is slowly happening here hasn't fully sunk in with the folks around which sometimes makes the shock of the beautiful too much to see 'cause you know it is fleeting, disappearing, dying. You know. Buses and cars slow and honk and the growing crowd whistles and screams as the yellow Yugoslavs watch with one laughing, then leaning, groaning the scaffolding wood above me as the conga beat and clapping and honking and whistling drown in the roars of the outgoing train. City life moving out of sync with the subway sound as the light turns green and beneath the tracks I cross with my fingers in my ears.

Like every day, the sleigh bells sing on the door as I come in hot and sweating into the smoke and AC cool to see all the just-out-of-college white boys sitting at tables right near her, stealing long looks while tapping their heels and toes to the jukebox thrash and now country Johnny Cash, drinking, whispering, grinning, with their young eyes rolling all over the pinup curves of her breasts, legs, and mouth. Every day. Every day I simmer, watch, and wait while trying hard not to. But there she is again, never noticing or perhaps not caring or maybe even liking the young attention like she did downtown, though I'd never say this out loud for what it may mean then twist then break. The questions she'd ask me. The lies we'd have to tell.

Holding my tongue, watching my temper, working hard

to keep to my part of our new bargain, I come in and sit like this and when I can't take it, turn quick to look at the lot of them. Their eyes scatter everywhere. The slow ones caught in my sights but now staring just past her out the window at the dancing little dark kids smiling and splashing through the shooting water sprays from the open fire hydrant right outside or today some following the stream of water down to the crowd watching the black-haired brown woman flamenco-dancing in red.

"Kendra."

I know she sees me.

Shifting slow in her seat. Tapping those red nails. Pretending my looks aren't bothering her. Part of her bargain. But her eyes. That's what got away from her; was the way you might sometimes get ahold of something she didn't want you to see.

Downtown she said she wanted to move up here. Was sure. Said it would be different. Would change things back. Us back. Breathe life into us by making it new again like it used to feel. But this is what we got.

I look at her.

I know she sees me.

"So," I say to her.

"Well," she says to the window.

She is part American, part Brazilian, and come winter you'd probably call her white, but with some soft mixings of some things not so white, so she doesn't look real white but sort of Sicilian olive, Philippino brown, Brazilian beige from the long summer sun which somehow made it easier on my mind. She didn't seem to worry or see but would sort of smile during my bad times when I pointed out the looks and stares and nasty things I was sure people thought then said in corners in whispers. "You're imagining," she'd say. "Are you sure?" she'd ask. "A state of mind," she'd say. "Paranoia," she'd say. "Medication," she'd say flat after three stiff martinis.

Sometimes she'd get in my head, get me going good for months at a time, and I'd get to stabbing myself with her types of questions, getting that paranoia question rolling around my head, trying hard to see how she saw it, writing this off for that and that off for this.

Other times it wouldn't stick and I'd get real angry, wondering if she couldn't see the truth 'cause she was trying to play the part of the foreigner. The Bahian from Salvador, from the mountains, from money, searching for the kinder ways through things, the high road, not caring to understand or bow to the very real and ugly things of here. I could almost respect that. Sometimes. Sometimes I thought things like this. Sometimes I wanted to make her see it. Mash her face in it. Stick it to her. Make her feel it like I did so she'd know and not say some of the fucked-up things that came out of her mouth. Though she'd lived only a time in Brazil, out at night on the town she'd put that fake accent on calling herself Brazilian to anyone who happened to ask. A Brazilian of the heart, she'd say, forgoing the time she'd lived in Hawaii and her crazy white American mother, whom she never spoke about like she was born outta the side of her father's head. Had to snoop around Kendra's stuff to find out her mother was white. I didn't understand and she didn't like to talk about it. Her mother. Hawaii. In all the three years. Not a word.

I've never been to Brazil or Hawaii and there's only so much you can get from books and documentaries before you have to start listening close to someone else's stories and so sometimes, though hard to believe, I just thought she didn't know or understand, or feel it 'cause she was rich. Sheltered. Naive. Ignorant. White. "Ridiculous," she'd say after one of my office stories, and then "Ohhh," she'd say, "No," she'd say, "People don't do that," she'd say, "Who ever heard of such a thing," she'd sometimes say when I told her about the eyes, or "It's not for other people to decide who we love," she'd say when I told her about the murmurs, or while holding my hand, "I love you, not a color," she'd whisper, brushing those lips over my ear.

For when she had me going, she'd remind me how she'd grown up smiling in Bahia with the sun and the waves, conservative with money, and good families believing in the very old Christian way that those who did not have did not have for reasons entirely within the bounds of their own control. The if-they-didn't-want-to-be-there-they'd-be-someplace-else kind of thinking. I didn't buy this and sometimes in our other downtown life, late in the night at the bar when I'd had too much to drink, though I wasn't supposed to, I'd get going good and loud anyway, trying to make her see the truth by way of the many evil people who'd drifted in and out of my life. None of it did anything but inspire that faraway look that meant she didn't care to hear any of my horrible stories on the awful things people did and had done, how that could affect a mind and make you be. "You get what you give," she'd say. "You reap what you sow." And she practiced what she preached in her own life, living without caution, trying to laugh and smile through just about anything, lightly touching anybody in any place in ways that made people smile and feel better and reach out and touch her, caress her, and sometimes get lewd and do things they shouldn't. Like they couldn't help themselves. Like they didn't realize. Men and women. How the world moved for her. The impossible stories she had.

But she'd say she wasn't scared.

Said it hadn't changed her.

But I knew. Could see it in the sags in her cheeks. In the fine lines growing from the corners of her eyes.

And when I got nervous for her and said something about her late-night long rides on the subway or about how she sometimes liked to dress, how she shouldn't do this and might want to think about doing that a little different from time to time, she'd only laugh and put her smile away saying, "I'd rather go back to Brazil than live your life of being afraid." I'd grit my teeth and take it but what do you say to that? What do you say to someone who won't listen? My beautiful beige bombshell like the magazines, like the movies, like nobody else, which made men want to do things for her and with her and to her, which she mostly tried to spin and smile with but couldn't these days for how it never changed no matter what she did. Sometimes watching her I thought New York might run her over. Other times, during my bad days, I knew it would be me.

And with the music going and the dying light coming through the café window in pieces, in shadows, I close my eyes and open them and watch her, hoping to regain what I once felt, feel how all those white boys must see her now, beautiful, fresh, and new, without the leaks and problems of time. I look at her and she's smiling at something and I try to remember her downtown naked and smiling and singing in the tub of warm water I drew for her 'cause I knew how she loved baths in any weather with her warm voice filling all the voids of our very empty new apartment with bossa nova and then old Brazilian folk songs. I sat listening in the hallway on the floor in the heat with closed eyes wondering how someone like me ended up with someone so special like her, with me, her with me, but there she is again trying to kill me now with that foot tapping against my chair to country Johnny Cash like everyone else in there, tapping like she's one of them, like it's all gone out of us and I'm no longer there. She knows I hate this.

"Kendra."

A subway coming.

She sees me.

I put my hand on her shoulder, slip it down to her leg, and she slowly slides her chair from me. Recrosses her legs the other way so now I'm reaching, looking like a fool. I pull my hand away.

"So," I say.

After a while.

"So, should we go?" I say.

"Where do you want to go?" she says.

"Someplace else."

"We talked about this," she says. "Do you remember talking about this?" she says. "Right at this table."

"I can't remember anything," I say.

"Don't mess with me," she says.

"Sure," I say, "I remember everything."

"Your tone," she says without that accent.

"Sure," I say.

"What are you trying to do?" putting that accent back on.

"Leave."

"I didn't ask for this."

"You must've," I say.

"No," she says, "I didn't."

"Who does, then?" I say. "Who ever does?" I say. "Who asks for the big plate of shit they get?"

She turns and looks out the window. Watches the kids, wet and laughing, screaming and smiling with bright faces, running around splashing. She smiles at the shiny girl with her face mushed up against the window. Outside looks so easy. A subway coming and you can feel it through the chairs.

"Well," I say, "are you ready to go?"

"What you're doing to me," she says. "How you treat me. How you talk to me."

I shake my head. Don't know what that means. Hope it'll go away.

We watch awhile. I wait. Shake my head.

Our lacquered table beginning to glow in the half-light. And then.

"It's true," she says, "it all changes," she says, "when you start dating them."

"What does that shit mean?" I say with their awful music going. "Who told you that, your shrink I pay for lead you to that?" I say. "That headshrink of yours," I say, "or is that what chapter twelve in your Dalai Lama happy book says, 'Don't you worry, Kendra, it all changes but turns out all right'?" I say.

"Not always all right," she says.

"Yeah," I say.

"Sure," she says in the same flat tone I like to use on her.

"Why do you make me sit through this?" I say.

"Nobody can make you do anything, Maceo," she says in her special way that gets me wondering how in the world I can pull off never going in there again, never going home either, erasing all of her forever from my mind and getting all my things into a little suitcase and disappearing forever into some tropical faraway place full of good, warm people a hundred thousand million miles away on some beach with a drink in my hand and waves on my feet smiling and free but no, here I am again with her and these people and their music, all of us watching her as she doesn't answer and looks away from me out the long window to the passing people and cars and buses, yellow cabs, shiny kids splashing, shirtless old men sitting in tree shade drinking slow, banging dominoes with half an eye on the beautiful woman in red dancing flamenco. Sometimes the kids stop and look at Kendra through the window. How she looks back at them too. She knows different now. But those days for us are gone. Gone, gone, gone.

Not for nothing did any dark folks ever go into this shiny new place, no matter what kind of deals they tried to throw in the window, 'cause they could see the white folks coming and wanted it to stop, but she'd be in there and nowadays didn't care and every day I'd come way uptown from work all the way downtown from off the train from down off the escalator into a different dark country, sweating all over in my summer suit, to sit in there and see if she might smile a little and really want to leave with me.

Dark folks of the neighborhood walk by through the

heat, slow, looking hard through the window at us sitting in there. I try not to catch any of their eyes, look up at green treetops, passing trains, pink clouds moving a little slower than tiny airplanes, or down at tree shadows, building shadows, shiny hubcaps catching pieces of the pink orange light.

In here I feel on the wrong side of things. A fool. Embarrassed.

And now embarrassed about being embarrassed. Why should it matter? I tell myself as I look over to see if she's seen me cringing, and "I don't need you to defend me," she says. "That's what we talked about," she says in the talking noise between jukebox songs, "I can take care of myself," with muted conga beats and kid giggles coming soft over the AC. "You can't control everything," she says, sipping some of her black cherry soda, "it's not for me you're fighting, anyway," watching the silver trains passing by.

Living down in TriBeCa, we tried to be positive and patient, calm and open, vulnerable and true, to talk out the swirling, empty things going wrong. Talked to friends, families, therapists, fortune tellers, the stars, our guts, each other. Talked of everything till there was nothing left to say. But somehow the words couldn't quite get around what was slowly happening to us, or the ways to stop whatever it was from every day swallowing us up whole. What is it to say something out loud? Not to do what you want to do?

After a while she just wanted to move. Thought it might help things. Change things, forgive things, make it better to move away from the them and that of downtown, the money and eyes, the half-truths and stories, the scene, downtown where at some party her best friend's fiancé quietly put his hand down her pants, downtown where her ex kept asking her to sleep with him and his new wife, downtown in those dresses, in those bars, in those clubs, with those smiles, hemorrhaging money downtown where I kissed another woman and she punched me in the mouth, downtown where we had an abortion in place of a baby I wanted to have, the puke-green walls of that Planned Parenthood, her sick, ashy face coming down that hall, hand on her belly, walking slow, hunched over from the weight of the shame and tears and blood, downtown, downtown, downtown, how they expected you to act, look, and be, give us a new beginning to be back in my old neighborhood around something closer to the color of us both, uptown here, where things were slow and different. "I don't know," I'd said, "place doesn't change people," I'd said, but she really seemed to know, whispered in my ear up here sitting on a stoop in the sun, "It'll all be all right," and I needed to believe if you tried hard, the good things didn't just run out of gas and die the way I guess they must do.

For at one time all of this, uptown, was the other end, the forbidden place, the black part of town where dark people from all over this country came to be something and wonder and watch all the proud others who'd made it, dressed sharp as tacks, stepping along beautiful as can be. A renaissance, they'd called it. A dream. But all of that was long ago. A different time. Lost. Now only majestic shells stuck about back streets between broken buildings empty and ripe for anyone from everywhere figuring hard on how to make a buck or save a buck while finding a big, cheap place to start a business or live. The renovated apartment buildings. The new white café. Their swanky bar up the way.

The kids I'd known here, before our family moved to Jersey, were black, grown and gone, and up here in doorways checking mailboxes, knocking and asking for the families from my old weekend paper route, like ours, not remembered, not known, subletted and elsewhere, absent landlords moved off and away to big houses and apartments out in the suburbs and other cities where we could play with white kids and rich black kids and our dark parents didn't have to worry about us getting mugged or beaten or robbed but new and different things nobody really knew of like trying to fit in where we would never fit in without losing something essential which we lost. Up here, at that time, there were some whites about the busy streets trying to blend in, maybe some sort of Chinese that stayed out of everyone's way but not enough of anything to raise any eyebrows, just enough so those around could look about and smile with the nice, soft salting of folks.

Back then, right when the ordinance went through and all the island folks really started filling those projects, a lot of people just left right off believing those people were going to drive down real estate value and bring the real city problems over into our neighborhood with their other poor ways from their poor island countries from across the street, tracks, and sea.

Muggings, lootings, drugs always there, now was them. Them. Them not understanding things and just crossing the street from their projects to our side, them sitting out on lawn chairs leering and laughing, them kissing after our women like my mother, them drinking beer from brown bags with their radios blasting salsa into the night, them making some money and not knowing any better than just to move over to where all of us lived and laughed, so the tracks up above no longer separated anybody from anything.

We had packed monthly community meetings in the Old Circle Donut shop deep into the nights where many light-colored black people screamed and yelled about what they were going to do to block this and stop that to make sure those people didn't come over anymore, changing things, but nobody could stop it and everybody somewhere down deep knew.

Even my folks got to thinking and arguing over the new Puerto Rican project people causing things, trying to push us out with the way they just came over to our playgrounds, our stores, like everything was all right and ours was theirs, asking questions and doing things, not speaking English and not caring they didn't speak it either. "This shit?" my pop would say. "These people and their goddamn shit," he'd say. "Went to Vietnam for this shit," he'd say, stepping along, "got shot twice in the gut and nearly died for this?" he'd say, and "No," he'd say, eating peanuts dipped in Pepsi, "no, no, no," he'd sometimes say, cracking walnuts in his hand, getting mad all over while opening our big window and looking out at them on our side of things, sitting out on milk crates and stoops banging dominoes and laughing and looking with their music going. Body tense like he wanted to scream. Muttering. My pop, who rushed straight ahead at an ambush in Cambodia and got his pack shot off. My pop. And when I got it the third time by thirteen early one evening by gunpoint in our elevator coming from the Red Apple supermarket across the way from some young thing, I couldn't

tell you now black, white, brown, Chinese, there my dad
was roaring into the night with his army-issue .45, screaming he was going to get them all, kill every motherfucker
out there, as my mother shook her head back and forth,
rocking me slow with her soft lips on my tears saying,
"We've got to move, got to go, got to leave," which made
even commuting from New Jersey and living around all
white folks into a seemingly better life to live.

But they speak the Spanish up here now. Everywhere.
The tiny Chinese joints splattered all around. The little
stationery stores. The cleaners. The liquor stores. Even
Jumbo Burger and the Old Circle Donut shop where
many of us would go early Saturdays and Sundays after
our paper routes with new money burning fresh holes in
our pockets to get some of the first doughnuts of the day
and watch Shazam and Chilly Willy on the counter TV
Mr. Ferguson had rigged up special just for us paperboys,
even the Old Circle Donut shop and Jumbo Burger, where
one night over ten not-of-his dollars bullying, big-mouthed
Nigel finally got his by way of a knife in the gut and like
some bad movie crumpled to the ground and moaned and
bled and died, even the Old Circle Donut shop and Jumbo
Burger were gone over into something entirely new. They
all had the Spanish with neon-scripted red, big and bright,
on their front signs and would speak it to you when you
walked in almost anywhere, as if this were some other
tropical country from across the sea. Or a big fucking joke.
They knew you didn't know. They speak the Spanish up
here now, while those downtown run bus tours all around
the neighborhood for foreign folks hoping to catch something of what it used to be, but only the hulks and shells of
dreams with a lot of people trying their everything just to

hold on while the others run around just as hard trying to push them on out.

A lot of folks around the neighborhood didn't like it, the many new people moving in up here, them here, really the young, rich, hip white folks up here and how they changed things with their shiny new café and swanky bar right up the way, come nights them downtown dressed up and walking all around anywhere, everywhere, feeling safe, and come days others like them snooping around trying to find some way of coming up here too. A deal. These days the police drove around slow and even walked around some in the day and parked sometimes in the night to stay here and there, eyeing you hard to check, watch, and see. Whites, kids, even girls, walked around everywhere talking loud and laughing, just-out-of-college white smiling college girls, real suburban blondes dressed the same in Gap tank tops and J. Crew sun skirts all over the streets at all hours of the day and night, in pairs even alone drunk and high like they were downtown, not feeling the glares, not noticing the old and young out on metal chairs blasting merengue and salsa dura, angry and watching, looking and leering, waiting with hard words that the white kids walking didn't seem to hear or care about or know to be scared enough to avoid.

They had monthly meetings at Taza de Oro, where they'd get red-faced mad shouting real loud and long about all the things they were going to do to block this and prevent that to get them to stop coming, to get the ones here to move on out. Old and young jammed into the hot, beat-up joint, sweating, red-faced mad screaming and yelling in English and Spanish about legislation and letters and senators and city boards and rising rents, restoration, revitalization, and

T-shirts, all the while knowing full well there was really nothing any of them could do to stop it.

With the many Day-Glo picket signs standing around the room, frayed, bent, and beaten like worn-out soldiers, Kendra and I would sit on metal foldout chairs in the very back, watching and listening. Many more signs than people and looking around, I could never figure what they thought was going to happen. How many more folks did they think they could stir up? We were new to this, sure, but all the time in there and very near the color of them and she spoke some Spanish and was beautiful and could nod and figure through the rest, so they weren't sure what to think. We understood. We wanted to support. She liked people who fought for what they wanted, for change, stood up for their beliefs. How she once believed me to be. And they needed the numbers. Come September and twelve more were to be evicted. Some funky cappuccino place had bought the old picture frame shop. The police were stopping darker neighborhood folks asking all sorts of questions come nights. And the daily protests were going longer and getting uglier with many more people marching and screaming, banging pots and pans with wooden spoons and forks chanting call and response with a Brooklyn Iranian activist they'd brought in special with a big megaphone. All of them scared now about losing their homes to the soaring rents and new people happy to pay those low prices. There was no more dancing. They could feel it close now.

And like all the rest anywhere, those men in there couldn't help but look at her, tall and curvy with big breasts and good curly black hair and those dimples with that smile and her Brazilian beige complexion and oval eyes so she could pass for anything anybody fantasized her to be. And she would smile back at them too. Downtown-smile like she used to do, like I wasn't sitting next to her, like I wasn't around, like I wouldn't know or she wouldn't care if I did, and there in that place they could feel that too. I'd look at her there downtown-smiling at everyone, anyone, smiling and nodding and nodding and smiling trying to soften the blows of their eyes and here's where she'd seem beautiful. I look at her and wish whatever it was would just stop so it could go back to how it was. But it never does. Nothing does.

"You gotta smile at every man in here?" I say. "This is what's wrong," I say. "Said you were going to stop this and stop that but you don't. Smiling at this one, looking at that one like you'd fuck him right here, and then you got the nerve to get huffy, wondering why people are all the time groping you, saying shit. Not saying they're right, it's just how it is. An ugly, simple truth. You get hit on when you stick your tits out and smile and lick your lips. Do that and folks think they got license. And what am I supposed to do?"

"I don't need you to defend my honor," she says.

"Sure," I say, "sticking your tits out is what it is, Kendra. That's the why, baby. Right here and now is the simple answer you've been searching all your life for," and "I see how you feel," she says flat, and looking at me and looking down, and somewhere somehow I feel better, knowing I shouldn't, knowing all too well I really haven't won anything beyond bigger problems to come.

And with her wide-eyed looking and no longer smiling, they really get their fire going up there at that podium like they can feel her deflate and want to puff her right back

up. The new one up there now with his white STOP THE
EVICTION T-shirt on and busted fat lip, talking while
touching his bashed-up black-and-blue eye, puffing out
his Puerto Rican chest, talking real loud over the subway
rumble and car horns, looking right at her while going on
and on in Spanish as clapping women turn, shooting her
dirty looks and glares, with Kendra there next to me hot
and sweating and again sitting up and nodding and clapping and smiling along when everyone else smiles and
claps along, looking right back up at their men pounding
the podium like they were big shots and really could do
something to make any of it change. The flamenco woman
now over there hiding her calves in starched deep blue
jeans, sitting up straight and proper like a lady with her
back away from the back of the metal chair and her long
black hair tied up tight in a bun. She stands, turns like a
ballerina but with a tiny sleeping baby cradled in her
arms. Moving toward the blond dreadlocked white boy
by the finger food who's been coming in here the past few
weeks not saying a word to anyone, with his every day
different-colored dashiki and now with her baby in his
hands, him smiling and cooing like he's the father, and
like that nothing in my whole wide world makes sense.
Many church fans spread wide and waving. Two big standing propeller fans humming and blowing a cross section of
breezy, warm air slow back and forth as I move in close,
close, close, almost onto Kendra's chair, her sweating arms
and legs sliding against mine. "What are they saying?" I
whisper in her ear, trying to regain some control, trying to
smile, trying to make the other things go away, my arm
around her shoulder, my hand on her leg.

And she pretends like she doesn't hear me, doesn't feel me, pretends like I'm not there. Knowing I shouldn't get so mad, trying to cool down my mind, and "Baby," I say, Kendra with her chest out and clapping and sweating, looking at the pounding fists, and everyone else there looking up at the one with the bashed-in face, up there at the podium pleading, talking fast, into it, feeling it, and heads careening around, looking at us all the way in the back real close. "What he say?" I try to say nice with all of them one on top of the other packed into the small joint, looking back and forth from us to the podium as the man screams loud and points at us all the way in the back and then to the dreadlocked blonde in the dashiki holding the baby as some leaning against the side walls glare at us and cheer sometimes, interrupt, pointing sometimes, everything loud with those up there sweating and talking above everyone and everything while looking at her and smiling and glaring at me, acting all big like they could do something to stop what everyone knew was going to get them no matter what they tried to do, and she looks at me like, Where are you going? and "Outside for some air," I say.

Back in the heat, and "What are they saying?" I whisper sweet, and she says nothing, not smiling. "What are they saying?" I ask louder above the fan and talking and flamenco mother trying to quiet her now screaming baby. "How they're going to fight to keep the gringos out," she finally says. "And . . . ," I say. "How they're going to stand up for themselves, fight the police violence in the courts, too," she says. "And now," I say. "How they vote like everyone else in this city. How they have rights," and I smile. "And what else," I say. "Things you don't want to

know," to me, her now smiling back out at them and at
the speaker, who's gesturing toward us in the back. "What
are they saying?" I say. "Learn Spanish," she says, and
"What are they saying?" I say, "Let it go," she says, and
"Who are you to tell me what I want to know?" I say loud.
"Because I know you," she says, now smiling at the ones
turning and looking at us. "Sit down," she says. "You're
the problem, you know that?" I say. "You're the reason for
all this shit," I say, "you don't stop," I say, "not one fucking
bit," I say real loud, realizing I'm standing, screaming,
sweating, looking hard at her and then anyone else turning to look at us. "What do you want me to do?" she says.
"You're embarrassing me," she says quiet, "They're saying you're a gringo, all right," she says, "that people like
us are the real problem," she says, and I look at my suit,
my tie, my too-expensive shoes, and "Sit down," she says
softly, "please sit," she says gently without that accent
with her hand on my sweating arm as I look around at the
staring, angry eyes and feel the quiet of the hot and sticky
room and the whirl of the big fans, and there's hardly a
noise, save the quiet broken by the flamenco mother lost
in her starched jeans and long-sleeved light blue blouse,
hiding her breast, up and rocking and humming soft nothings to quiet her cranky baby. All of them looking at us in
the back. At me. "I told you how people are," I say, "I told
you," I say, "Look at this," I say, "Look at them," I say,
"Try and help and . . . ," but Kendra only looks down and
turns her head for a window not there.

She never went again.

After that, in this hot, humid heat, most of the men from
the meetings, in long pants and white socks, *guraveras,*
colored fedoras though the heat, would look at me and

then smile big at her, whistling soft, saying, "Guapa, guapa," with their rolling eyes moving all over her up and down as she looked down, trying not to see or softly smile as I tried to look them off but never could. And what, was I going to hit an old man, a kid who didn't know any better? No. And so they'd just smile at me, wink at me, as we went walking by. The women would turn their heads like we weren't there or stare real hard and stop talking on a word, slowly, quietly watching us, with loud, sharp Spanish words and laughing to our backs. "What'd they say?" I'd ask impulsively, but she wouldn't answer, head down, pretending I hadn't asked or she didn't know, which maybe was best like she'd said in the first place.

I'm not sure why I'd go but I'd go and I'd go, skip the café, take my suit, shoes, and tie off and go and they'd look at me strange in one of their STOP THE EVICTION white T-shirts like I should know something I must not know or maybe did know and didn't want to see, me there in the back among the Day-Glo signs near the finger food and drinks, standing very alone near the door in that heat not understanding, trying to clap along with everyone else, kids squirming in between legs, but they'd point and glare and gesture and sometimes laugh, so after a while I couldn't take the looks and stopped going, too.

EVERY DAY. ALL THESE PEOPLE. ALL OF US TOGETHER, stuffed hot into smells of old sweat all through this rocking car, everyone side to side and back to back, standing over one another, with everyone standing so you can't move left or right, bodies rocking and shaking, all moving as one as the subway goes back and forth, nothing but bobbing heads and many black and white hands holding on to the warm, long silver poles, my back all hot and wet, soaked through, my front wet in circles and spots, hot and choked up in here like my old man once was, with my summer suit on like he used to wear and my shirt undone a little with my tie stuffed down deep into my pants pocket, and off the subway as sweat rolls down my back and legs for the real heat of the outside sun and baked station. I step off and stop and take my wet suit jacket off, wipe my forehead, put my handkerchief away, and stop and wonder at her and what she says and thinks and will say today as the many of them all move rushing and pushing and shoving through me on past, methodical like a slow, rushing herd to the stairs, me just standing, watching, sweating, thinking. All are down the stairs. Another train coming, not stopping, and I put my briefcase down and my face clear and broken in the windows passing at the speed of light and it's gone. I look and a brown boy down the way leaning over the platform with a green beer bottle above his head in his hand looks at me and smiles and throws it down at the white cops in their blue police car down below. A loud bang but he's already down the stairs. I look as another subway is rushing toward me. I know what I have to do. I go down too and the big black woman inside the token booth is screaming, "English, English," to the brown woman with a baby screaming back in Spanish things I don't understand as her baby kicks and cries in the stroller as both brown and black scream and scream which grows softer as I go down and down off the escalator to the hot sidewalk sweating all over real good now, as red and white police lights spin and reflect around the shop windows below the invisible rails as the white cops have a different brown boy up hard with his hands behind his back, his body pressed tight against the dented blue squad car as the roaring trains rattle in and out and salsa loud from somewhere as brown picketers with tired Day-Glo signs begin to gather around behind the white cops as trucks and buses and gypsy cabs slow into one lane, heads turning, rubbernecking, and watching to see what's going on as rattling trains roar and car horns blare and idle bus engines cough black exhaust as the gathering mob begins to say things loud, so I can hear them over everything as the heat comes down and the warm sweat drips down my back, front, and legs as I walk slow wondering and thinking past the shooting water sprays and dancing dark kids running all around laughing and splashing and into the whoosh of their AC cool where she is sitting in her corner by the window in an orange summer sundress waiting for me. I sit down. She doesn't look at me. She's smoking. A crumpled soft pack of American Spirits by her soda. The sweat all over my body feels cold.

I know what I have to do.

"The light's perfect," she says, and it is as the setting pink light is making long shadows of the trees and buildings onto the sidewalk and street, the light reflecting off the bodies of the slow passing trucks and cars, off the windows of the bodegas, Chinese joints, beauty salons splattered all around, the rose orange light on the silver rushing trains racing up and down, back and forth, uptown, downtown. Orange rose like her dress.

"Like your dress," I say nice, setting it up and she smiles and the lines in her face. "There's something I need to tell you," and she looks up at the tin ceiling and down at the polished wood floor and I feel cold as a little rumbling at our feet and she's looking at me. "You're home early," she says, and touches my hand with hers, puts her fingers through mine, and "What's all this?" I say, and "Complaining about this, too," she says sweet, and with her nail softly scratching something off the side of my face, touches my cheek, "No," I say. Behind her a white girl's shirt rises a little up her back and a small triangle of yellow lace underwear, a tattoo of ivy going down, and my girl turns and looks and then looks at me looking and I don't try to hide it.

"What are you trying to do?" she says.

We sit for a while with their music going on loud as the light is going gold. Rush-hour trains keep passing pink outside and inside across the polished wood floor through the redbrick wall, over the lacquered tables, in circles big, then small, through our pint glasses as above on the tracks they quickly rattle in and slowly rumble out. We sit and say nothing, watching and listening to thrash music and roars and car horns and bus screeches and truck engines and loud, angry screaming from the direction of the police cars as many more sirens come closer and many more red and white lights flash in all the store windows right across the way, with white eyes watching us, watching her all over. I don't turn to see, though. A few of them go to the door to see where all the screaming is coming from but we don't move. I look at the one right behind her with the ivy down her back and her lacy yellow underwear and wonder about her and the feel of something new. Kendra puts her cigarette out in what's left of her black cherry soda and it hisses and moans. She looks up at me looking all around, trying not to look her in her eyes.

"It's beautiful here," she says, "can't you see?" she says, watching me. "The subways, this light," she says, "can't you see?" she says with that phony accent all gone, pointing at the orange rose subways floating on the floor. "The sounds," she says with one really rattling, and "No," I say as brown people stream down to the sounds of the mob as I cringe, trying to disappear, and "Do I embarrass you?" she says.

"I've been thinking a lot," I say, "thinking hard," I say, "and I guess maybe if you were black. Just culturally, Kendra, I think if you were black, I mean, it would make everything so much easier and—"

"What are you talking about?" she says. "I am black and—"

"Or if I were white, probably if I were white like you, I guess. My mother once said she wished she were white, and I didn't understand and she kept talking on and on about how much easier everything in her life would've been if she were just a plain old white woman, how she could be invisible like a spy, how much more she could've attained, how many doors would've been open to her, and I didn't understand it and we argued about it for years, but now—"

"What the fuck are you trying to do here?" she says as black and brown folks stream by the big window screaming at things we can't see but know as the roar of the mob is getting louder above the sounds of the many more sirens and beat cops racing down the way to stop them. I realize I'm staring, watching it all.

"Do I embarrass you?" she says again.

"To have something easy," I say.

"Do I embarrass you?"

"Easy without outside troubles."

"Suppose I said that to you?"

"Easy without any worries."

"You're a fucking heartless coward, is what it is. Like you've been all your fucking life," she says, and I feel it and she looks away.

"That's what May said," I said, and she looks at me. "Your friend," I say, and she looks at me, "and I thought in my mind," I say, "I thought I might maybe go away for a little while," I say to nobody, "maybe Brazil to learn more about you." I smile, lying to the floor, "Just for a little while," fooling nobody, "just to clear my head," lying to myself.

"Do you want to go?" Kendra says.

Got her.

Out the door.

Her long skirt sways back and forth against both knees as she slowly walks through the heat in front of me past the dancing kids, who stop for a moment and look at her and then go on, past the many screaming people near the cops with the brown boy now in one of their cars, past the soft whistle of "Guapa" and the white girls in tank tops with Popsicles walking and the old men in fedoras watching on stoops, playing dominoes on crates, up and up toward our building. The light is orange and pink, reflecting gold in the windows in the tops of the buildings up along the other side of our street, gold in all the projects looming above everything. Shadows of the black wrought-iron fire escapes on the sides of all the buildings like lace.

The light comes through her skirt and I can see her long legs naked beneath the swishing fabric. The people look some as she walks a little in front of me, walking slow through long tree and stoop shadows. The street busy and loud with merengue and moving and shifting and white folks walking here and there away with us from the big mob as the light sinks into different colors for the haze. She walks with her head down and forward as I walk slowly behind.

Upstairs, inside and into the bathroom, holding her hair as her back heaves up as she vomits. Back in the living room and I go to turn the lamp on, and "No," she says, and I go for the air conditioner, and "No," she says, to close the curtains, and "No," she says, "no need," she says. I go to the bathroom and run the bathwater, panicking, and back and watching her in the quiet and the living room is getting dark and is very warm. She takes off her tank top and then her sundress and naked falls into the couch. "Do you want anything?" she says. "Something to eat?" she says, not looking at me.

"No," I say.

"All right," she says.

"You can have a bath," I say with the water running, and "No," she says, and I realize what I've done.

Lights come on yellow in the buildings across the way. Curtains close.

"Do you want me to close the curtains?" I say.

"No," she says.

"People will see you," I say above the overflowing water sounds from the bathroom, and she looks at me and gets up in the coming dark and sits in the window naked with everything out for all to see, "They'll see you," I say again, "those people," I say but she just sits there and sits there and sits there, not moving, eyes out and looking as the night darkness slowly comes in over us, swallowing everything in the room as the gradual sounds of the roaring trains and sirens softly drift in and then like nothing quietly wash on out and by.

A LIE IN SEVEN PARTS

1

NOBODY EVER WANTS TO TELL A LIE BUT THE LIES JUMP
up on you, force themselves through you, out your mouth,
off your lips into the world and once they're out there
they're out there and what can you say, what do you say
to the one you hope to love, "That's not true, what I just
said"? "That's not true what I said last year"? Can't do
that, can't do that with the one you want to have and
hold, tell her, tell her it's all a lie, that last sentence you
just said that sounded so sweet but had no relationship to
the truth. No. For the good, once they're out there they're
out there and it's no longer yours for the fixing.

But love, huh. Lust, huh. *La doce amor,* as the Brazilians like to say. Sometimes it's better like that. Sometimes
that's what it takes. What the adventure calls for. What
people want to hear. Need to hear. A warmed-up story to
smooth things. A sweet little lie to ease things.

At night, in the dark, I raise up in bed as she moves so
quietly I hardly hear her footsteps across the carpet, her
hand brushing along the wall, slow swish of her legs, low
hum of the ceiling fan, warm air blowing through our

window, ice cubes tinkling the big glass of water she always brings to bed on these hot Brazilian nights. I close my eyes and listen hard for her though I know I can't hear all her light shuffles and wall caresses as she comes to me waiting in bed. My tall, little-bosomed, mocha-colored German with a funny English accent, purple toenail polish, blue gray eyes, and slender silver rings on all her cinnamon fingers, with a little silver stud like a glittering tiny mole in her small little nose.

It was her back I saw first. Ada's back! Broad and tan in an open-backed orange dress that let you see the swimmer's V all the way down, disappearing into dress around her ass. It was her back, that delicate turn, those blue gray eyes quickly looking down and up me and then that smile. That long stare and smile so you knew. That stare, that smile, then her hands back down around the older, graying blond man with no real business holding her, hugging her, loving her. Hans, his name was.

At the Bahia airport, luggage coming out Brazilian slow, blue gray eyes winking at me, smiles covering me as I'm waiting for my big blue backpack to slide down the chute so I can begin my next adventure in this mysterious land I'd heard so many all over Brazil and New York speak of, I remember looking at her and looking at him, blond and smiling in this sea of brown, and I knew, could see clear, how things could maybe go.

But a lie never goes away. Lurks around you. Stays with you, sticks on you like this hot, humid Brazilian night and roar of voices from the many bars, from the cobblestoned square, floating on the wind, soft through our window, washing over me, through me, sitting here in bed waiting for my love to come to me in the dark, smiling. A bed built on lies. It was a lie that made her leave him. A story that keeps her here. A lie that keeps us going. Lies that keep us smiling. Lies, a woman with a beautiful back, and a magical piece of land they say watches you, keeps you, judges your every move. It's all kept me here seven years now. Seven.

2

MACHIAVELLI SAID THE BEST WAY TO RID YOURSELF OF the one you despise is to be right there whispering in his ear giving counsel. Lying next to me, she looks at me and tells me, like she sometimes does before bed, it's fate that we are with each other, and the other, her old one, her old love, Hans, she always says frowning, Hans, she says, is gone. Fate. "Remember how we kept seeing each other all over the city? Everywhere. At Novo Tiempo, at Shangri La, in the ocean, along the beach, in those days when you were the only man who could truly make me smile and feel not lonely. Imagine. An American." "Destiny," I say, and she tries to smile and I smile at her and nod with her and pull her close with my arm around her waist telling her I love her, which, that part, is true. I never ask about the others who I bet even now still cover her with wide smiles, long probing hugs, innuendo conversations about the great feats they have surely mastered if she would only like to try again and see. She never asks me how or why. Fate, we say.

My plane was late leaving Rio and late landing in Bahia and on adventures you don't carry a book but chase your

heart so I strapped my big blue backpack on, watching
them, standing waiting, walking, me quickly getting behind them, close and near them and that back I needed to
touch, her sweet smells, the line of muscle in her calves,
and *amor*, ahhh sweet *amor*, and slowly out the sliding
doors into the thick, warm night and in the next cab and
"Vamos," pointing at their black cab speeding off in front
of us. Seemed right. I was ready for something else. They
seemed like the doing-things-trying-things sort. A good
Carnaval pair. Like they had class, like they knew what
they were doing. Were after adventure, experience, and
that back and those eyes and how easy to follow the one
you love, your heart, to get rid of the German you despise,
when you see them leave each day, can watch with leisure
where they go, watch what they like to eat, don't like to
eat, watch what they like to do late in the night, see it all
for yourself, all the good and bad things up close for yourself. Like Nietzsche said, one must "outwit chance and
lead it by the hand."

3

IN PORTUGUESE *PELOURINHO* MEANS "WHIPPING POST."
All around the narrow streets, all about the large cobblestoned square, rusted iron rings are still embedded into
the thick stone walls. In the old slave days, with the smell
of urine, blood, and sweat soaking the narrow streets, the
rusted rings were used by the whites, who looked like
him, to chain and beat and whip and torture the stripped
black backs of the Africans, who looked like us. That first
Tuesday night, the three of us walking down together,
holding hands to not get lost through the great throng of

la gente, the loud people everywhere jammed into the cobblestoned square of Pelourinho, you could smell only the
big black old women of the *Candomblé* religion dressed all
in billowing white dresses with big, white turbans covering their hair, you could smell only their grilling shish
kebabs and *aracaje* frying in the *dendê* oil that came
straight over from Africa. The big women moving mouths
and hands, tucking money away, shifting, smiling, laughing, stirring *aracaje* batter, selling cola, water, and *guaraná*
soda from dirty Styrofoam coolers from out on the edges
of the square as Oludum in red, gold, black, and green
dress up on the old slave auction stone stage with their
ten drummers swinging in unison as four horns and two
saxophones blare out the melody as the people, the hun-
dreds of swaying coffee- and toffee- and mocha- and cocoa-
and cinnamon- and chestnut-, walnut-, peanut-, pecan-,
caramel-, chocolate-, fudge-, cappuccino-, almond-colored
black people, fill out all of the big square moving and
sweating tight and close as one to the different steps of
these songs that have been passed down for generations.

With the music all around everywhere, off the pastel
buildings, Ada immediately got out there into it. Into all
of them there moving. Her standing still and smiling in
the middle turning here and there closely watching the
women move and step, and then Ada there slowly trying
and soon shaking and moving like she was one of them,
like she was born here, her hands and head, everything so
the many Brazilian men, even some of the younger, well-
built *policía*, came up on her, touching her with hands on
that beautiful back. Their hands all about her twisting
body while moving their Brazilian moves on her and then
behind her, moving with her as one with everyone up on

stage and everyone else in the square in time, in beat, to the banging African rhythms, in the similar steps that have been passed down from father to son, mother to daughter. Ada's closed eyes, shaking hips, bouncing feet, moving breasts, fifty different smiles for fifty different folks. You could tell she liked them watching her, coming close, touching her. Her looking over at smiling Hans. I'd seen things like this before. She liked to do things, try things, trust people, throw her head back to laugh and let go. Watching her there moving and smiling, getting groped comfortably in the name of dance, you could tell a good dose was in her, too. Love and lust. Desire wrapped in lies.

"You should try," I urged Hans. He was watching her very closely. "Everyone is friendly," I said, hoping to get him in there.

He tried it too. They watched him but watched him differently. Tall. Gangly. White. Blond. Off beat. Off-kilter. Old. Like a cliché. A big joke. She paid him no mind and then was over somewhere else making lovey eyes at the young, well-built men up dancing on her. They seemed to be having very big problems, Ada and Hans.

Even the young *policía*, the undercovers, who did not dance with anyone, were there moving, touching her to the music. Song after song as she let her head back and laughed, closed eyes, smiling, getting everything right. Hans watched, standing still in a moving wave with arms crossed across his chest, eyes fixed on the band Oludum moving the crowd like magic from the stage. He didn't seem to see her. Like trying too hard not to care. They didn't seem a very happy couple. Later I remembered having said to him, "Will we ever understand the ways of women?"

"They are worst than we," he said, and I nodded, "but it makes no difference," he said, and I nodded at this, too.

Tuesday nights—sometimes the day and the night, traditionally the nights, though—the slaves had to themselves, and they honor that still, here, in one of the most mystical places in the world, Pelourinho, Salvador, Bahia, Brazil.

"Bahia," they say here, "is more African than Africa," they say. There they moved and changed their customs, here "she," they say, "she the land," they say, wouldn't allow anything to change. Things now are right like they were then, right when they got off the boat in chains except now no chains you can see. Understand? Different ways to bind. No? No one else in all the black slave world fought to keep their customs like they did here in Brazil, in Bahia, in Pelourinho, the black ghetto, the soul of Brazil, the navel of the universe, the most mystical place in the world.

Ada looked Bahian Brazilian, being mocha and in the ways she moved to music, and I'm sometimes black as night and speak their language. And he, well, he stood out. And they watched him. Where after some time we all were together some nights, where up over there, above all the sweating, moving, dancing people, at the top of the cobblestoned slope, where Oludum banged and swung sweet melodies every Tuesday night, at one time one of the largest number of slaves in the free world were bought and sold and sent long, long ways away. Free black Africans sold and worn dead for sugarcane. They say this was the sometimes first stopping place for the broken survivors who'd been spooned up in those devil ships for months. They say some of their ghosts, the ones chained and flogged and killed, still linger around the square, waiting, wanting, watching. They say they were done in by those who looked like him. Nobody forgets that.

All good and bad comes full circle for those who watch and wait. And around here that comes wrapped in soft smiles and patient eyes. Those two would come smiling down the cobblestoned streets from white Barra where we all stayed in the big hotel to see black Pelourinho where the teenage boys and teenage girls and women and men and music and fun and adventures were. Seven nights in that hotel could feed a whole town for half a year. But the road of adventure to help consequence sometimes has a high price. Down here we all could feel the energy of good things and possibilities. At least, she and I could. He wanted to and seemed set to try.

4

BRAZILIAN PORTUGUESE IS A BEAUTIFUL LANGUAGE, THE most beautiful in the world with its movements and tones and up-and-down rhythms in soft *ish*es and easy *oohh*s, so even in Pelourinho, in the cobblestoned square, up on the cobblestoned slave stage when the fruit and vegetable man screams early in the morning when the heat is not so strong, and there's still a slight mist in the air, even when he screams, "Frutas, laranjas, macas, peras, mangabas, melancia, verduras, bom alface," he sounds like he's waiting for the drums to begin beating so he can break into the song he has already started to sing.

I'd been in Brazil a long while and loved Portuguese and they loved it when me, an American, an American dark as night, spoke their language with them. They said it showed respect toward their culture and always that night I'd drink for free or get something extra with my dinner with a pat on the back and a pleasant smile from the manager or owner or whore or waiter waiting on me, especially in Pelourinho, the black ghetto of Bahia, where they didn't see non-Brazilian blacks too often. They would look at mocha Ada and speak to her in Portuguese and she'd smile, turning red, not knowing what they were saying, look at me as they looked back at her, "Não falla Portuguese?" They didn't speak to blond Hans, which was just how I figured. They'd do that and he'd just stand there and smile with his camera, maybe take a picture as they smiled with easy eyes right back. I had followed my heart which had followed *amor*, which had followed the adventure of them to the many churches and beaches here and there, aimless around Barra and finally into Pelourinho those first few days before I was ready to introduce myself over Brahma beer in the Novo Tiempo bar on the edge of the square.

I'd seen the looks they got, him tall and pale, gray hair cut close on his head, with his rich man's shiny watch and little digital camera he used for snapping pictures of very young girls and very young boys, smiling street kids in rags, women dressed in near nothing, regular people walking around Pelourinho doing their day jobs. The looks they gave him, taking pictures and then holding beautiful, broad-backed mocha Ada. "Smile," he'd say at them. People didn't like it. Didn't like it at all. Didn't like a white person like that with one of ours, one of ours that was so fresh and young and pretty. My little flower. They didn't like it and said as much when I asked the bartenders and shopkeepers and waiters who watched them going around laughing and smiling, without a care, walking down the cobblestoned streets of our ghetto, in the afternoon heat, sweet mocha Ada glittering and tall, swaying those sweet hips in those long, open dresses, with the flash of those long legs, her turning and watching you up and down with those voodoo blue gray eyes everyone seemed to lick their lips talk of and crave. "Bom dia," the men would all say sweet, waving and grinning and smiling into singing the first few lines of their favorite love song as she passed, swaying and smiling, looking right back at all of them. She was beautiful and knew too well how to use the great jolt. The woman's weapon to make men melt. Melt and do things men would otherwise never ever think about doing. One has to be wary to execute a good plan.

5

THE TRAVEL GUIDE ADA AND HANS SWORE BY WARNED travelers not to go down into Pelourinho at night alone, for it was dangerous with all the brutal street crime and *policía* beatings and random rapes and everywhere street orphans who with outstretched hands swarmed and bumped and begged you with many fingers quick and gentle through your pockets, stealing it all. With the red pen I'd given her special she must've circled that in red. With the two of them off to the island Morro de São Paulo with some drug-using awful Argentines for a few days and nights and a story accompanied by a few dollars and I had a very polite and smiling bellboy and my own magnetic key to their suite in a white envelope beneath my door upon my return from my daily swim in the rooftop pool. They say haste is a precept of the devil and leads only to ruin and the best enterprises are those that are carried out slowly with caution. So I took my time because you never want to hurt someone who doesn't very much deserve it. I wanted to make sure I was getting one of those slimies who are all the time slipping somehow through the grip of justice and not some poor bastard who didn't know any better.

Things were going well, yes, but you must be sure and certain, which requires taking heed of the many details of the plan.

I went in and turned the air conditioner back on to cool it down some. Turned the stereo on which was tucked in a deceptive cabinet looking like all the other furniture in there. Zeca Pagodinho in the disc player. The next CD Oludum. Oludum soft throughout their suite a little above the sound of the AC. What a view they had. Much better than my room. But beauty always gets best. Separate beds. I lay down where she must lie, because you could still breathe in her lingering perfume on the two pillows. I took the pillow to my nose. Yes. Closed my eyes. Dreamed of her, thought of things, plans, devices, what I could do to those dirty, conniving Argentines of Hans's, always licking their chops, eyeing Ada. Then I began smiling some, thinking what we might do, she and I, her willing, of course, if things turned for the right. I got up and took my time touching this and that, feeling the soft satin things to my face, lounging in their chair and her bed, out on the terrace, back in, now looking good and hard for something that might help me see things clear to the end.

Their guidebook did acknowledge Pelourinho to be one

of the better places in all of Brazil to drink and get a true feeling for black Brazil. That was circled in blue. He must've done that. Going through their room in hopes of finding something more than my very good hunch and intuition to fortify my assumptions. But besides some pictures of children he'd been taking indicating, to somebody with an eye for it, the direction he was heading, there was nothing too concrete or obviously alarming. Just ugliness to those that cared to look and see it. Someone once took pictures of me when I couldn't hardly do anything to stop them. Losing my cool wouldn't help things, though. Physical violence doesn't sting and stay the way a good, calculated plan does, doesn't leave the right and lasting footprint. Anyway, I knew this wasn't going to be easy or nice. A person like him. Doing so much to hide the truth. With his Tom Cruise million-dollar smile. A despicable man with a Hollywood grin. That's how these types get away with so much. Who suspects the someone looking so fragile and kind and helpless? When it happens with a one like this, it's almost beyond comprehension to those who don't know how to look. But I knew. Good lessons need to simmer awhile getting nice and hot before a person can truly come to understand and see how far he's strayed from the right. How much he's truly hurt people. How much he's going to have to pay.

The argument soon became should they stay or go. He wanted to discuss it in private. Ada said loud she'd nothing to hide. "Do you have something to hide?" she said. He said he'd nothing to hide.

Like a little kid, Hans said he was now not enjoying the time anymore. I think I heard "dangerous" out of him

many times. She, of course, was. She had many secret suit-
ors. I'm sure. A place like Salvador is very kind to someone so pretty. It was stalling matters between her and me.
The men. All that attention. The way they went after her.
And her wandering eye. The way she would smile at them.
The jolt she let out. I knew better than to chase a broken
twisted beauty like her. Knew watching her dancing that
first Tuesday night in the square. But the heart never lis-
tens how it should and I was lost, for all of this had become
something else entirely. I knew.

Anyway, the Argentines. The high-flying drugs. His
"personal explorations," as he called it. All part of it. Hans
wanted something new. Something different. A little safer,
too. Maybe for a moment he too saw how this place could
be when you didn't tread lightly, didn't treat it respect-
fully, but things had come too far and his sort of thing had
gone on too long and needed to be stamped out decisively.
See, out with his Argentines one night, and then off wandering, looking for his things by himself, he'd run into
some trouble and been mugged a little bit. Hit a few too
many times for his liking. A slight problem. An overzeal-
ous player in the plan. But that camera and those pictures
he was taking. It wasn't quite right. So who could blame
anybody for doing more, for going further than was asked
when they saw something like this? Not me. His camera
was also taken for good measure.

So come the next day, lying on towels with the burning
sun down the Bahian coast on some beach watching the
turquoise waves coming in and going out, he leaned over
and apologized for having to go away with her for a while
to try and sort things out, maybe decide where they might

want to go next to be truly comfortable, "Maybe away from here," he said, "just she and I," he said, "someplace remote," he said, "away from all of this."

"Of course," I said, "it's the only thing that would be right," I said, "we've all been there in need of quiet time and space to help us figure our things out," I said, "but of course I hope you two find a way to stay. It is a beautiful place if you live it right," and he patted my shoulder.

When they came back from their little island trip, not so happy with the Argentines now, who probably made the suggestion to go in the first place, he still wasn't so sure but I pushed and prodded him on the foolishness of guidebooks and the cold and altitude of Bolivia and the fun of Carnaval right here in one of the best places in the world. "Calm yourself," I told him, "be careful," I said, "and you'll be able to enjoy the wonderful drumming of Oludum and the dancing crowd and soft smiles and easy eyes of the generous people here," I told him. And I can't tell you how persuasive that Ada can be when she wants something very badly. Told him to remember that first Tuesday night when we all went out together and thought everything so fine, fresh, and new. How much fun we had. "You saw for yourself," I said, "never trust a guidebook more than your gut," I said by the rooftop pool, "there are great secrets in this city beyond any persons writing books," I said in lounge chairs, in the hot sun, over drinks. "And when you got hit and harassed, you knew you were not in the safest place for that time of night alone, Hans. There's not much over there and I can't quite figure what you were doing there anyway," I said, and he looked at me. "Oh," he said. And she looked at him. "I was very drunk, you know. I got lost coming back," he said. "Well, there. It's easy not to get so drunk and lost," I said. He still couldn't see. Blinded by his own bullshit. So I went on, "We'll go out together next time. Just you and me for a while and they'll come to know you better down there and we'll be a little more safe with how we drink and you'll never have to worry about something like that again," and he seemed to smile and she looked at his scabbed nose as his black-and-blue puffed eyes roamed thongs and naked sand and white-colored breasts. He nodded his head. "Would you like a beer?" he asked us. His pale, pink body moving over past the first bar toward the second bar near the very beautiful brown woman quietly sunbathing in the nude on her back. Ada shook her head. She'd grown used to him. Used to turning a blind eye. I wondered why she just wouldn't leave him. I wonder that today.

"Safe for us?" she'd said softly that day.

"I wouldn't lie to you," I'd said quietly, leaning over maybe too close, back. "I've been here a long time and it's true once they get used to you down there—that is, see you come and go, talking with the folks living down there—they accept nearly all good people," I'd said. "Are we good people?" she'd said. "Good enough," I'd said. "Besides," I'd said with the salty wind and hiss of the ocean waves from far down below, "besides," I'd said, "in this country you've gotta worry more about the police," I'd said, "or in your case," I whispered, "the strong, young policemen who always seem to have plenty of time for pretty young foreigners that seem to enjoy strong young men in uniforms," and I winked as she blushed, looking toward Hans, and then beyond him, out over the railing at the never-ending sapphire sea. She was thinking things, too.

They made arrangements to stay.

After some weeks he'd come to enjoy going down to the square with just me while leaving Ada at the hotel for the night. She never said a word about it and he didn't have any suspicions or worries or cares leaving someone like her cooped up at home, like I most certainly would've and did. She knew things though. She knew but let it go. Sometimes looking at her, watching her, the things she said, her games, I thought her smarter than us both but that's not a good way to think about the one you love, hope to have and hold. Anyway, leaving her in the big suite alone reading some Brazilian magazine, *Veja*, "She'll be fine," he'd say, "and isn't it true, sometimes boys have to go out by themselves and be boys?"

"Sure," I said.

"I'm on vacation," he said.

"I know," I said.

"Now she feels it," he said.

"Yes," I said, "yes, to find amor," I said, "we must sometimes go out to do these very difficult things," and he laughed his big laugh and smiled his million-dollar smile and then put on a very dignified straight face like we were friends and I'd find anything he said not reprehensible, "Yes, it is very true," he said, patting my back and smiling a little less big now, hopefully realizing who he was smiling at. Someone that knew. Was onto him.

Down there in the square, in the bars, the bartenders and bar owners and waiters and waitresses would talk to him and smile and give him drinks when he was with me up at the bar, down sitting at a table. He liked that, too. He liked to drink. He liked to drink very much into the night and get red-eyed drunk and look without regard at all the Brazilian women and teenage boys and teenage girls walking around dressed in very little, there fingering his new camera around his neck. It would nearly turn your stomach to see. At the tables with him there, they'd be all around us sitting and laughing and smiling and drinking, pulling on his collar for his attention, trying to make conversation with him as if we were all old friends and nobody wanted anything special from anyone.

"Ahhh, amor," I said one night finishing the last of my *guaraná*, about to take my early departure from the many at our table as had become my custom over the weeks and he pulled me back down into the seat and for a moment there I thought maybe he might know something but he only began smiling shyly, looking down, saying soft like a little schoolboy nearly turning red with embarrassment, how he liked taking assorted chocolates most outside in the open fresh air. I smiled back at him. "Most people do," I said. He grinned. He liked that very much. I told him not to worry. I told him it wasn't such a big deal and I'd take care of everything for him, if he needed me to.

Lying on her side of the bed, looking far and deep out at the Atlantic the way she must do, flipping through the pages of their guidebook, making marks with my own red pen. It also said, for those inclined, almost all of the whores in Bahia were in Pelourinho in all the bars where he and I would go. You couldn't tell they were whores until they asked you for a small donation for their time. Hans's guidebook advised all inclined to such things to wear a rubber times two, for Brazil has one of the highest rates of AIDS in the world.

Going all around the nooks and corners of their suite I never once saw any rubbers or anything in the drawers and toilet bags and closets and luggage, worn pants, creased pants, purses, under the mattress, in money belts tucked away, you name it, everything, for I figured a man making a habit of doing these sorts of things would have to have a supply of extra-strength, well-made German condoms stashed somewhere safe, for in the figuring I didn't count him to be that much of a fool, 'cause such a thing could ruin everything for everybody. My delicate flower, wilted, bruised, and poisonous. No. I even asked Ada. "He hates using anything," she said as I held her hand with concern at the table very late one night at dinner, as she smiled. "But I'm all right"—she smiled and winked—"nor do you need to worry yourself about such things just yet," she said. "Excuse my worry," I said.

Anyway, lying there, I circled that rubber stuff in red. Circled it many times and had to restrain myself from doing it again and again every time I wandered in there fact-finding. You can warn somebody only so many times before you must let it fall out of your hands.

6

THE CRUZEIRO. THAT SAD, SAD CURRENCY WITH AN IN-flation rate of more than 100 percent a month. Brazilians are aching for hard currency to keep their heads above the starving line. The dollar. The pound. The mark. People will resort to bad things when they're faced with being hungry, with their children going hungry, with getting thrown out of their homes and who can blame them? Circumstances make people do what they do, are forced to do, and who can blame them for the choices they have to choose from? Need and want make people do what they do, are forced to do, and who from the lap of luxury can justly judge and blame? No one blames a lion for devouring an antelope. Or the hunter that kills that lion to protect his own. A smiling blond German looking for that kind of fun with a pocketful of marks? Easy.

At the bars without Ada, Hans would buy drinks for all the Rastas jamming to Bob Marley and Alpha Blondie, for all the pretty girls and winking women and boy whores and girl whores smiling our way, for the waiters waiting on us, for the shopkeepers, tourists, drug dealers, thirsty, hungry, and anyone else in there, for that matter. I'd pull my wallet out, and "No, no," he'd say in our big group, touching my hand in a way I asked him not to, "I insist," and "You're too kind," I'd say smiling, "we're becoming such friends," I'd say, him shaking his head like it was nothing now laughing comfortable believing himself to be the life of the Novo Tiempo bar.

Weeks of this and people began to smile big and toothy when he came around with me and they would come and sit with us and try to speak German to him, laugh at him in Portuguese, as he shelled out mark after mark so everyone in the bar could get good and loaded while eating till their heart's content. Got so he'd almost go down there alone without having to worry about getting mugged for all there knew they'd get their share of what they wanted and why bite the hand that feeds? Everybody knows that.

Hans had gotten into other things there, too. Stronger things. Things I don't like to think of or discuss. Humiliating, cruel things that wore out even some of the worst of them there in Pelourinho who needed the money most. Unspeakables to make the skin crawl. Operation stories.

Things that made it hard to look at him many of the days. If you were to believe the stories. Of course, they knew he had the money and could afford anything and he was so curious. It kept him out very late and soon even she didn't even care to ask for the obvious lies he'd tell. He meant to make his point. A kid let free in the candy store. His true colors. I think of it all as justice.

In Brazil, in Bahia, in Pelourinho, nobody has any money and the women with nothing are no fools when they see a foreigner with a pocketful. An English or German or American could take their whole family out of poverty just like that. *Snap.* They think we're all rich. Just during the last Carnaval, in the rain, watching a *bloco* parade, I had some grandma offer her thirteen-year-old granddaughter to me to do with what I liked. She said, "Muinto bom," winking and grinning and pointing at her granddaughter shaking her little thirteen-year-old ass for her life right in my face. Dollars, marks, and cruzeiros.

The favela women up in Bahia were much worse off than anything. He knew it and would smile. I smiled too. Told him I'd thought about it and the best place for sweet *amor* with chocolates outside was on the opened top floor of the hotel out by the cabana out by the pool, late in the night, when you could smell the salt strong in the fresh ocean air. He smiled, and I told him he must go late, after they'd closed off swimming to everyone. "For the cabana," I said, "the pool cabana," I said, "has no roof, save the stars and the dark sky, with a big window overlooking the sea where you can both look out, as I hear is how you take your preference these days." He winked at me and I went on, "The window is always wide open to take in the breeze. It is very nice," I said. "A special place," I said, "my place," I said, and he looked at me. "Yes, it's true," I said. "And nobody ever goes out there," I said, "and it is very dark without light so nobody can look in and see even if whoever they are taking some of your pictures, snooping around, chooses to look for you," I said. "Very nice," I said, "I know firsthand," I said, "and even if Ada is in your room she would never find out, not even look, not even suspect you in such a place, for Bahia is so full of magical things you could be doing with all the new people you've met, if you need say something," I said, "say for your sociological studies back in Düsseldorf," and I smiled and winked how he liked. He stroked his gray blond goatee and thought another hotel would be safer but I explained what more he could accomplish with those whores and whomever else by impressing them with the money of where he was staying, the best place in all of Bahia, alone in the pool cabana with nothing over him but the smell of fresh air and the many stars in the night sky. They would very much want to perform, I said, "because they are people, too," I explained, "subject to the same sorts of persuasions as any other regular woman." I said, "You must remember that when you want to do your special things." I told him, and he wavered a little, "And when will you ever have this chance?" I told him, "When in Germany will you ever have such a pick of so many assorted fresh and different chocolates? Cherry filled, caramel covered, the dark, dark ones you like so much?" and he smiled at me, "Yes, it is quite an opportunity," he said, and I winked at him how he liked and smiled, dropping a set of keys to the pool gates into his open white palm.

At the bar they would all smile at him too, when he would leave early with his newfound Brazilian candies.

7

AUDACITY, ADVANTAGE, AND CONSEQUENCE. IT NEVER ceases to amaze me the things people do when they think they won't get caught. How brave when their feet aren't to the fire, when the tables aren't quite turned, when they don't see retribution creeping on them fast from behind. How they smile all the while taking advantage. Their audacity in the art of humiliation. Stepping on others' backs. Upon people's necks. Eating and sleeping, making love with great passion. Holding their kids, looking one directly in the eyes, sincerely shaking hands, these people, watching TV, reading the paper, drinking, loving their wives, walking here, going there, free of guilt, free of fear, laughing out loud without any decent shame. Just like you or me. You've seen them. These people. These bad people. They're everywhere. Lurking in the daylight, hiding by walking tall. Some people try to tell you about divine justice. The day of reckoning. Nonviolence. Patience. Karma. But sometimes that's just not good enough. Takes too long. Doesn't penetrate. Isn't felt. Isn't appreciated. Makes nobody change. 'Cause in the end who really knows what happens to the bad ones? How many actually slip away into smiling, comfortable lives? That's the real question. As for me, I like to see things through to the end. Make sure. Bring consequence. Help and guide it along to where it truly fits best. You aren't always blessed with the chance, but ohhhh, when you are . . .

Yes, I took Ada out. I took her out a lot. I don't fuck whores or want to watch anyone else doing so. Not for any money in the world. So I'd go running back to the hotel to see Ada whenever I could and sometimes she'd be there and many times, I'm afraid, she was not. When she wasn't there I liked to believe she was mostly alone wondering at the many new friends Hans had and how much of Bahia they were trying to show him. I'd like to believe she took strolls alone along the long beach, hoping to meet someone else, longing to be with someone who would treat her how she should be treated. Someone who would appreciate her. Love her. I have to believe that now but I guess that makes me some special kind of fool.

Then too, back then, he'd long stopped touching her, giving her all sorts of stories why, and I consoled her as much as an outsider should—well, a little more, to be perfectly honest, 'cause everyone needs attention, needs true loving, and I was around and alone to give it, so I did. She and I liked each other from the start and you have to be careful in this world. Careful with the precious people.

So the big night we came back and things were going well, according to plan, and like always those days with my arms around her in the elevator. Holding her, feeling her, and up to the top floor with the outdoor pool and the fuck noises, what fuck noises of pain we heard as soon as we opened the glass sliding door to the patio of the big outdoor pool on the roof. She smiled at first, looking at me with big gray blue eyes and I said, "Someone is working very hard. I'm sorry about this but people in love," I said, "maybe we should go someplace else?" I said, and she giggled a little, trying not to, and "I'm not sure I still want to swim," she said, "but why should it bother me?" she said. "Amor," she said, smiling, and "Yes," I said, smiling back and louder noises and a man's voice talking and her face was not smiling so much now and I went to talk and she put two fingers over my lips, metal on flesh, and she looked at me and I frowned like I didn't know, and she motioned for me to open the gate and we walked in, slowly, quietly, over past the cabana door, with her walking faster in front of me. And we leaned down, putting our ears to the closed cabana door, listening, wondering, considering, and I stood up, shook my head like I was completely unsure of the other side and what and why she was doing this and I, pointing over the railing, in a whisper, "Here is the view?" to her, who had her ear down pressed to the door listening to nothing, nothing but darkness and quiet and the some-times smack of the black Atlantic Ocean waves on the sand far down below that she now did not want to see and a voice full of soft *ish*es and easy *oohh*s struggling with English and then another low laugh and the loud noises started up again and Ada's mischievous grin, now smil-ing, frowning, biting her lips, whispering, "The shit! It cannot be true." Her hands waving me to open the door slowly, slowly, and a door thought invisible in the dark but not invisible or dark for someone with *amor*, dollars, and a plan, was opened.

A nice dinner and a lot of good wine and a pleasant walk toward our hotel and European politeness and hold-ing hands and smiles and good conversation on the beach and the suggestion of the beautiful Atlantic Ocean view from up high and maybe a late-night swim, with my arm around her waist, hand resting on her hip, in the elevator, a kiss in that elevator, a kiss and a smile, and a giggle, a walk, a wonder, a listen, a whisper, a frown, a horror, sweet beautiful horror as a door went open wide to unveil for everyone to see through the half-moon shadows, right there in our faces, two chocolate hands cuffed, with someone else red and sweating and fucking away in the pool cabana on the top floor of the most expensive hotel in all Bahia. Whips, cuffs, chains, and cellophane, screams, shouting, tears, pleading, red faint flashing lights of the warning buoys out in the black ocean out the big window overlooking the Atlantic with fresh salty ocean air softly blowing some papers next to an open jar of apple-green jelly lube to make it all slide nice and easy. They stopped. The young teenager with nuts and now breasts too, smiled best he could. We all stood in the dark and watched one another. It was one of those long and pregnant moments when you end up wishing for the rest of your life you could've said something. Something really good. Poignant. To sum up the sadness and madness of it all. Something so Hans knew and could feel it how so many were forced to and not just 'cause he was caught and beaten badly at his own game but because he truly understood how many people he'd done in, one way or another, for doing the *fun* things he could afford to do. I stood there horrified like the rest of them. But nothing came out. Not a single word. Not a human sound. Silence. And then the soft crashing waves down below coming up and in through the window opened wide, through the roof opened to a watching half-moon and blanketing crowd of two million billion bright stars. Seeing the keys in the half-light, I went over and un-locked Milton and he rubbed his wrists. He picked up Hans's camera, tripod and all, and threw it out the win-dow. I still run it all through my mind. Over and over. Every day.

Oh, sure, Hans tried to say I set him up but all those things don't get heard when you get caught naked with a very big hard-on fucking on some poor mutilated teenage whore who's at that very moment cursing at your girl-friend for fucking up his chances to get out of the ghetto, off the streets, and be rich, or at least make the little money promised to hold him and his family over the short while he had left before he took his last bows in this round of life. Ada didn't like that part of it either. She didn't understand what was being cursed at her but she didn't like any of it, first covering her eyes with all her silver-ringed fingers, then both her ears, sort of weeping, saying "Too far, too far" and "God" and "Jesus" in English, almost like someone had told her her part in the great grand plan as I can see Hans again wonderfully screaming and threaten-ing me saying Maria as he was calling him, wasn't a whore and how Maria wanted to become like this and such lies like that, now turning to Ada, him butt naked on his knees cowering, crying, clawing at her white blouse, pleading in that nasty German for her to listen, listen, how he had a problem and how he'd go seek help back at home but she had her hands over her ears, eyes shut tight screaming "My God, my goodness" over and over like that, no matter what he was trying to say and you could tell that was clearly the end of it for those two. Not even when he stood up and screamed and grabbed her hands away from her ears then grabbed me so I couldn't writhe loose, told me to tell the truth about all the things that had happened at the bar, with him not really wanting to try this stuff, did I flinch, did I flinch or blink.

"Tell the truth," he said with that filthy accent, and I smiled and told him I didn't know what the fuck he was talking about, and that he should know better than to try and take advantage of poor women or men or transvestites, or little girls and boys, for that matter, doing anything and everything just to try and stay afloat. "Responsibility," I told him, "you people need to take some responsibility for once."

Ada started screaming right as I was getting going good on the hows and whys of it and about those pictures, my goodness, those pictures, though he didn't seem to be listening but grabbing Ada, so I pushed him over off his knees and told him to leave her alone and put his clothes on. Ada saw that, liked that, stopped screaming, put her head in my chest, her arm around my waist, like she liked to do. "We have love," she said to my chest in English, "la doce amor," she said in Portuguese as Milton sorta smiled and Hans, wide eyed, shook his head no, no, as I started stroking out the curls of her long black curly hair, smiling over at Hans naked with his pecker hanging down low in the shadows way over in the corner. "It's true," I said loud to everyone, "everything she says is true," my hand going up and down the V in her beautiful swimmer's back, "it's amor," I said, kissing her cheek.

Milton didn't like any of it but did like it when I smiled at him and told him in Portuguese not to worry, telling him I would give him the rest come Sunday. Hans didn't like any of it either. Didn't like any of it at all. Just sat there naked, in the shadows over away in the corner on the cabana flagstones, head drooped, palms covering eyes, mouth making moans, head shaking back and forth, every now and then looking up and over at me, smiling real big and toothy at him with Ada's head in my chest and my hand helping to console her tears by moving through her hair, kissing her forehead, and then letting my hand glide up and down that beautiful back.

8

IT'S A STRANGE THING FOLLOWING YOUR HEART THROUGH to the end of an adventure. Even with the best plan you never know what will happen and what you'll say next and how people will react to such things. I love Ada and that's mostly true most times. I don't fuck whores and I don't leave her home at night and I get drunk, sure, but with her too so she doesn't feel lonely or left out, feels included in things, knows I'm not doing things all over here and there like her last one. The people here love us and treat us well most of the time and don't mention anything about the quick exit of the German who had a cockload of diseases whether he knew it or not. A parting gift that gives *you* the very short shelf life. No one mentions Ada's decision to stay in Pelourinho with me. They just smile at us, nod and smile and wave and watch as we walk on by.

A bed full of lies that stick on you and never go away. Sometimes late at night when the wind's blowing soft and the people in the bars are laughing and singing and the fan has the easy whine and the ocean air is full with salt, I sit up in bed with my fingers running back and forth through her long curly black hair thinking that maybe some lies aren't so bad, some lies are worth the telling, worth the telling and their secrets worth putting away forever for the keeping.

ABOUT THE AUTHOR

Nelson Eubanks grew up in New York and New Jersey. He played soccer in Barcelona, Spain, for Sant Andreu before receiving an M.A. from the University of San Francisco and then an M.F.A. from Columbia University. His story "Uncle Raymond" appeared in the anthology *Mending the World*, edited by Rosemarie Robotham. This is his first book. He lives in New Orleans where he is at work on a novel.